Wifey Status:

Renaissance Collection

Wifey Status:

Renaissance Collection

Racquel Williams

www.urbanbooks.net

Urban Books, LLC
300 Farmingdale Road, NY-Route 109
Farmingdale, NY 11735

ISBN 13: 978-1-62286-616-8
ISBN 10: 1-62286-616-9

First Mass Market Printing December 2017
Printed in the United States of America

10 9 8 7 6 5 4 3 2 1

Distributed by Kensington Publishing Corp.
Submit orders to:
Customer Service
400 Hahn Road
Westminster, MD 21157-4627
Phone: 1-800-733-3000
Fax: 1-800-659-243

Wifey Status:
Renaissance Collection

by

Racquel Williams

Dedication

I dedicate this book to my three sons: Malik, Jehmel, and Zahir. You guys are the sole reason why I get up every day and push forward for greater things. I know we had a rough patch, but it only strengthened our bond. Thanks for loving me unconditionally. I love you guys eternally.

Acknowledgment

First and foremost, I want to give all praise to Allah for seeing me through all trials and tribulations and for his continuous blessings.

To my mom Rosa, words cannot explain the gratitude that I feel for you. Thank you for being there unconditionally for me and the boys.

To Leon Mcken, thank you for being there when I needed you the most. I'm forever grateful.

To my husband Carlo Brownlee, three years ago Allah brought us together for reasons beyond our understanding. I'm blessed to have you as my partner as I journey through this life. I love you.

To my bestie Sophia Newsome, it's been twenty-six years of solid friendship. Thanks for having my back through thick and thin, good or bad. I love you, girl.

To my brothers and sister: Shaun, Marvin, Martin, Rohan, Chris, and Tiana, I love you, guys—just wished we lived closer to each other.

To my father Martin Williams, thank you for making the effort to play a role in my life. You proved it's never too late to make a wrong right. Let's keep moving forward.

To the Trice family: Ma, Keisha, Bo, Shaun, and June, thanks for accepting me into your family. Love you, guys.

To my grandma Rosalee, thank you for making it possible for me and my family to have a better life. We owe you big time. I love you.

To my BOP family, guys, y'all have walked the walk with me. We cried together, laughed together, now let's celebrate together. I made it.

To Latoya Foote, girl, thank you for all those hot meals that you cooked me after a long day of writing. I've found a friend for life.

To Christopher Lee, thank you for being there at the lowest point in my life when I needed a friend. I will always have your back for life. Stay down; your day's coming to get your shine on.

To the ladies at Danbury FCI and all my homies in the feds, I learned that the race is not for the swift, but for those who can endure it. Stay down, stay focused. Allah has the final verdict.

To all my family and friends in Jamaica, Canada, and the UK—too many to name but you know who you are—I love you, guys. Thank you for your love and support. Now get out there and support your girl!

To Annemarie, Dana, Angie, Vanessa, Shuan, Tamirra, Shunetta, Christina, Dora, Darece, and all the ladies that I met along my journey through the feds, thank you for touching my life some way or another. I love you, guys.

To Treasure Blue, my mentor and big bro, thank you for being there when I needed advice on turning my dream into reality. I am forever grateful.

I want to say thank you to Hood Chronicles, Chrishawn Simpson, and the W.H.A.T! family for all their love and support.

I want to shout out all the authors that supported me on this journey. Y'all too much to name, but I am grateful.

Special shout-out to all my readers and supporters, I will forever be grateful.

To everyone that I failed to mention, charge it to my head and not my heart.

Chapter One

Sierra Rogers

"A closed mouth doesn't get fed." That's the motto which I lived by daily. A chick like me was hungry for the glamour life that regular bitches only dreamed of. I knew I was from a different caliber the second I, Sierra Rogers, entered this wicked world.

I was born and raised in Creighton Court Projects in Richmond, Virginia. My hood was known as one of the grimiest hoods on the city's East End. The niggas that repped Creighton were known for wreaking havoc all over the city of Richmond.

There were three types of folks that were eating well in my hood: the hustlers slinging them rocks, the stickup kids that were robbing the drug dealers, and the whores that were selling their pussy.

Life was hard from the get-go; I had to fend for myself at a young age. I got hip to the fact that Momma was a certified crackhead from the terrible things the kids would say to me on the playground and also hearing the dope boys cussing her out for their money.

I was a little over seventeen years old when Momma decided she'd had enough of being a sorry-ass parent. I remembered coming home from school and seeing two garbage bags packed with all the clothing she owned. I didn't bother to ask no question; this had become a regular stunt. She'd disappear for a few days, and then pop right back up without explanation. I winched as she planted a kiss on my forehead.

Somehow, tears welled up in my eyes, and I opened my mouth to say, "Momma, don't go," but the sounds never came out. Who was I fooling but my damn self? I couldn't wait for that no-good bitch to get on about her business. Then I could finally get some peace and quiet in my tumultuous life.

As I think back on how much I hated that bitch, it made my stomach turn. Lately, she was getting on my damn nerves with all that pacing back and forth that she did when she was geeking off that crack. And I was definitely sick of all the different tricks she'd brought home every night. I'd put my head underneath the pillow, trying my best to block out the disturbing sounds. The thin wall that separated our bedrooms wasn't enough to shield my tender ears from being exposed to hearing all the fucking and sucking that was taking place in the next room. That goes to show the little respect that Jeanette Rogers had for her teenage daughter.

This time was different though, 'cause it's been five years and four months, and Momma was still MIA. I couldn't help but wonder what the fuck happened to her. Then again, the bitch didn't give a flying fuck about her only seed, so fuck her!

I became a sole survivor; didn't have the guidance and structure that a young female growing up in the project needed. I made a mental note that I was going to get mines at any means necessary. I was blessed with a banging body. Five foot five, 143 pounds, proportioned out in all the right angles, skin as smooth as a newborn baby's ass, and a cute face. People say I resemble Nia Long, the actress. I believe my most valuable asset is my apple bottom ass. It's like a *Bam!* in your face kind of booty. Hmm . . . I hate to sound conceited, but I'll be the first one to tell you, I'm every nigga's dream and every bitch's nightmare.

I wasn't attracted to the younger heads. I've been around them long enough to know their MO. All they wanted was to hit and run and tell their boys. I skipped over the flunkies and headed straight to the top niggas in charge; they had nice rides and long pockets. With my sexy body and my sharp mouthpiece, I had no trouble reeling them into my life. This popping pussy got me not one, not two, but three high-paid sugar daddies taking care of me financially.

See, the thing with an older hustler, if you are a chick with a tight pussy and you are fucking and sucking him the right way, he has no limit on how much money he spends on you. That's just a way of securing the pussy so you won't fuck the next baller that's trying to get in.

As I got older, I knew that even with a nice body like mines, I would need something to back it up. See, pussy was like an elastic band; after a little wear and tear, it loses its grip. Plus, I didn't want to become a statistic—young, black female knocked up having four or five different baby daddies. Hell, nah! I was striving for the top spot—wifey—it was that simple.

I enrolled in Johnson's Beauty School on Second Street, and eighteen months later, I got my beautician's license. It didn't take long to secure me a chair at one of Richmond's most elite spots, International House of Beauty. It was a full-line salon. I knew the owner, Charley. He was also from Creighton, so he happily took me under his wing.

I took my skills to the shop and started killing it, from finger waves to Chinese buns and quick weaves. I even had something for the guys too. Living in the projects had its upside because bitches stayed broke all week, but always managed to trick the money up to get their wig fixed on the weekend, just in time for the club.

Alijah Jackson

I was born a hustler. Since the age of two, I was hustlin' Mom-dukes for five dollars to takin' bottles to the shop for the refund money. I even hustled the old heads for ice-cream money.

I knew that I had unique skills growing up, 'cause when boys my age were out playing soccer or baseball, I'd be pushing a handcart filled with mangoes to the nearby market. I'd get my grind on. It didn't matter that I was missing out on hanging with my homies, 'cause after a long day at the market, I headed home with a pocket filled with money. I'd hit Mom-dukes off, then placed the rest underneath my mattress.

I was born and raised in Tivoli Gardens in Kingston, Jamaica. Most refer to this area as "Tha Garden." Don't be fooled. This name didn't come about because all the flowers that were planted there; it's more like all the bodies that were droppin' due to the brutal murders that were taking place.

Crime became part of our everyday living. Murders and robberies became regular news in the community. A lot of people lost hope a long time ago; some turned into bums, while others turned to drugs and alcohol. The younger heads turned to selling drugs or slinging guns.

My mom happened to be one of the lucky ones that didn't become a victim of her environment. See, Mom-dukes ain't no slouch. She wanted more outta life for us, so with the help of family, we moved to the land of freedom—the Great USA. We moved to Mount Vernon, New York. Life was a lot different from back home. My mom got her a job which allowed us to keep a roof over our head and save a little for a rainy day.

However, crime was the same. The corners were crowded with the thugs tryin'a get their hustle on, and I became fascinated with the niggas that were slinging dope and driving flashy rides and getting all the bitches. I knew that'd be me one day. I dropped out of school and started working on my illegal mentality. I saved my allowance up, and at sixteen, I copped my first eight ball of crack for a buck twenty-five. I got cool with Darryl, an older cat that lived in my building. He was already a vet in the game, so he schooled me on how to cut and bag up dimes of crack. It didn't take long for me to get the hang of things. I went from copping eight balls to ozes in no time.

I was shocked at how much paper we were making in that small-ass town. We became partners and had Third Street and Fourth Avenue on lock. We found us a connect in Harlem that supplied us with that butter crack that had fiends running back for more. We became hood superstars overnight. Biggie ain't never lied when he said, "Mo' money, mo' problems."

Niggas started hating on us. We got into beefs about who controlled what turfs. I wasn't trying to hear that shit, and knowing I wasn't no stranger to gunplay, I laid a few of them niggas down.

Other problems came about. Niggas started to snitch, and since I wasn't no fool, I knew jakes (police) would be in pursuit real soon.

I was knee deep in the game and wasn't ready to stop just yet. I made the move from New York to Richmond, Virginia. It turned out to be a blessing, or more so a curse. Cats kept coming up top bragging 'bout how much paper they were making down South. I brought it to my boy's attention, and when the opportunity presented itself, we jumped on it.

I put a couple of niggas down with us, including two cats I knew from the Bronx, Chuck and Dre. They're cousins from Edenwald Project. Before I put them on my team, they were creating havoc all over the streets of the Bronx. They'd robbed and killed just to get their points across. Then there was Markus; he's the quietest outta the crew. He isn't no killer; he's more of a Wall Street-type cat. He kept my paper straight, and he was loyal to the cause.

My intention was to make this my town. I kept my eyes and ears opened to the street. That's how a star player like me rolled. The South turned out to be everything that was said, and more. I kept Julio as my connect and was killing the streets with that no-bake crack.

A lot of cats tried to holla at me, but if I wasn't feeling them or knew of them, I wouldn't give them no play. Bitches also tried to get in the mix, but I was fully aware of dudes getting set up by a sexy bitch. I would converse and trick a little, but once they started to ask all the damn questions, I'd turned ghost on their ass.

Chapter Two

Sierra Rogers

I strongly believed in destiny. When I met Alijah Jackson in 2006, it came as no surprise; our paths were already in the making. I met him one night at my job. I'd just finished on my last head of weave, tired as hell. As I looked in the mirror, I thought to myself I couldn't wait to get home and soak in some bubble bath . . . but before I could finish my thoughts, I heard someone push the door open.

I turned around to face a tall, sexy, chocolate brotha standing in front of me. I began to ask, "How'd you get in here?" but I was stuck on his appearance. Furthermore, it was my fault; I left the door unlocked.

"Hello, may I help you?" I spoke, looking this stranger dead into his seductive, bedroom eyes.

"Look, ma, I'm tryin'a get my hair braided."

"I'm sorry, hon, we're closed. Would you like to make an appointment fo' tomorrow?"

He stepped closer to my face. I felt like he was invading my space, so I took a step back.

"No disrespect, ma; I'm tryin'a get it done now!"

I wondered who the fuck that nigga thought he was. He got me fucked up.

"I said we're closed, so could you get yo' ass on out, so I could close up and head the fuck on home," I spat. I turned to walk to the door hoping he'd be in pursuit, but I be damned. This ignorant-ass nigga took a seat.

Yo! Truth be told, there was something about his in-control attitude that I was turned on by. After minutes of arguing back and forth, I finally gave in to his demand. I didn't bother to inquire what style he wanted, which I knew was unprofessional, but I didn't give a fuck at the time.

"Yo, I'm charging you fifty for the hair and fifty fo' my aggravation." I stretched my arm out, the whole time mean mugging him, but he didn't flinch.

"Bet!" he said without hesitation. He reached in his pocket and pulled out a stack of cash. After counting out four crisp fifty-dollar bills, he handed them to me. It was more than I asked for, but I wasn't complaining.

After several moments of complete silence, he spoke up and asked me my government. I didn't want to come off ignorant, so I told him my name. He told me his name was Alijah. I didn't want him to think I was pressed for his conversation, so I left it at that.

It took me 'bout thirty minutes to finish braiding his thick, long hair. I couldn't help but imagine what it would feel like to run my fingers through his hair while he did me on the sofa. That's when the little voice in my head said, "Bitch, stop trippin'."

I handed him a mirror, and that was that! He seemed satisfied as he thanked me and walked out. There was something about this dude that caught my attention. I noticed his swag, and he walked with cockiness. I walked over to the door and locked it this time. I pretended like I wasn't watching him, but I saw when he jumped into a truck with chrome rims on it. My curiosity got the best of me. I couldn't wait to find out who the fuck he was.

As I got in my car, I thought, *Boy, I'm beat.* I cut the radio on to Power 92 FM, Richmond's hottest radio station. They were playing some old-school reggae. My thoughts switched real fast to ole boy. I was feeling him. I peeped the way he was dressed. He had on a Coogie outfit and was iced out in a matching chain and bracelet. I know I was being nosy, but I could smell money from a mile away. I also sensed that he wasn't from around here either. His accent sent chills up my spine when he spoke. It was sexy as hell. Shit, I might be his future baby mama. Lmao.

Without further delay, I got out of the car and hurried into my apartment. I quickly undressed and jumped into the shower. The water felt so damn good on my tired body. After a thorough wash in Oil of Olay body wash, I felt like a brand-new woman. I got out of the tub and grabbed a towel, but before I could wrap up, I caught a glimpse of my body. I rubbed my hands across my 38DD breasts. I wondered what his hands would feel like over them. I hadn't been with a man in over a year. I was well overdue for some good loving.

I put on a Victoria's Secret boy shorts set, made me some hot chocolate, and got into bed. Picking up the remote, I thought maybe I could catch an episode of *Forensic Files* on Court TV.

Alijah Jackson

It wasn't no coincidence when I rolled up in the salon. I had my eyes set on one of the stylists up in there. A week ago, while riding down Nine Mile Road, I peeped shorty. She was standing outside. The first thing that caught my eyes was her phat ass. I had to make a U-turn to make sure my eyes weren't deceiving me, and sure enough, it was there in front of me. She was a little cutie too. I scoped her out from head to toe. She was a bad bitch from what I could see. I wanted to pull over and holla at her, but I was riding dirty, and I couldn't risk getting torn off in the name of a chick. I watched as she walked back inside, where I assumed she worked 'cause she had the little apron on.

A few days went by, and I couldn't get this chick off my mind. I rolled over to Fairfield Projects to rap with my homeboy, Saleem. He's a Muslim cat from Harlem. He moved to Virginia a few years ago and was doing pretty well for himself. He had Fairfield Projects on lock with heroin and coke.

If anyone could tell me what I needed to know, it'd be him. He was standing outside when I pulled up.

"Whaddup, son," I greeted him as I pulled up beside him.

"Peace, my brotha," he said, stretching his hand out. We exchanged daps.

"Good, get in; lemme rap wit' you real quick."

He got in without hesitation.

"Yo, B, let's get sump'n to grub on. I'm famished."

"Dats what it is then," he agreed.

As I made my way uptown, we didn't converse much; we were both lost in our own thoughts.

Saleem has always amazed me with his laid-back demeanor, but underneath, I knew he was capable of doing some serious damage.

As we entered the restaurant, I walked toward the back to holla at my boy Country, the owner. I then went back out front and placed my order. Saleem already placed his order, which was always seafood. I respect the brotha didn't eat no meat, but, shit, I sure love me some meat. I ordered a large rice and peas and oxtail. The order was on the house, so we got our food and left.

As we headed back to the East End, we discussed a little business. We both had the same plan to take over Church Hill, the city's most profitable drug area. We decided to put our minds together and get shit accomplished.

"Yo, Saleem, fuck these country-ass muthafuckas. We goin' try talkin' to the nigga in charge, at least try to work sump'n out. You feel me?"

"Brotha, that sound good, but we might have to strong-arm the spots and be ready fo' war," Saleem bragged.

"B, I'm ready fo' whatever."

"Alijah, this is a new ball game. Keep in mind you are not on your turf. Be careful, my brotha. Trust no one and always go with yo' first instinct." He placed his arm on my shoulder and then continued to rap.

"You're like a brotha to me. I would hate for anything to happen to you. Don't fall victim to the game," he said, and then removed his hand.

"Word, I feel what you sayin', son, but you kno' me; I'm on top of my game."

He didn't respond. Instead, he turned his head toward the street. I turned on his block to drop him off. Dang! I almost forgot my reason for the visit.

"Yo, B, I need a favor too."

"Spit it out."

"There's this shorty that I'm diggin'," I said.

He looked over at me. "She must be special."

"Nah, at least not yet. I'm tryin'a figure out who she is."

I gave him the lowdown about the other day. He kept smilin' and noddin' his head.

"Yo, son, I need to find out what clown she fucks wit'. Not that it matter 'cause I'ma take her from duke," I bragged.

"I understand. Give me a few hours. I gotcha!"

"A'ight. One."

He got out of my ride, and I pulled off.

Within hours, I got the news I was eagerly waiting on.

"Speak to me, son."

"I got the info you want."

I listened attentively to everything that holmes was spitting, and when he was finished, I closed the phone with a big Kool-Aid smile on my face. I was happy that I was alone. I could sit back and relax. I needed a plan, a way to get at li'l mama.

I never had problem getting at a bitch before, but this time was different. I shook the feeling and got up. I was gonna just walk up in there. I was *that* nigga she would soon realize.

I purposely waited until all the customers and workers left from outta there. I walked in and was thrown off that she wasn't on point of her surroundings. I sat in my ride for 'bout an hour scoping the scene out before I entered the salon.

I gave her a bullshit-ass story that I needed my hair braided, which was half true. She must've believed the crap that I was dishing out.

"We're closed. You need to make an appointment," she said.

I came close to saying, "Fuck this shit," but being the nigga that I was, I let her know I wanted it done. I got so close to her I could smell the apple candy on her breath, which gave an instant erection. She had a look on her face that expressed that she was feeling some type of way, so I took a step back.

After going back and forth, she finally gave in but decided to tax a nigga. She must didn't know money ain't a thing. If she played her cards right, she won't have to worry 'bout no money in the future.

She was sexy as hell when she pouted her full set of lips out. I asked her name just to break the silence. She answered in a fucked-up tone, but I wasn't stunting that. I already knew her name.

When she finished my hair, I was impressed with her work. I was gon' make her my personal stylist and bitch soon, I thought without a doubt.

"Good lookin' out, ma, I'm out." I walked out before she could respond. Putting my swagger on, I walked toward my brand-new truck. Then I glanced ova my shoulder and saw her peeping through the blinds. As I drove off, I smiled to myself and uttered, "Gotcha!"

Chapter Three

Sierra Rogers

I woke up in an upbeat mood, the wonders a good night's sleep could do to a person's mood. I was feeling myself, so I cut the stereo on, turning to my favorite song on Ray J's latest CD *One Wish*. I started to sing right along with him.

I went into my closet and grabbed a pair of Rocawear jeans and a wife beater. I hate to rush like that, but I had to hurry. My first appointment was Ms. Shirley, and God knew, I wasn't trying to hear her mouth about me being late again.

I got dressed in no time and checked myself out in the mirror. I applied some MAC lip gloss as I stepped out into the beautiful spring day.

Things went smoothly with my two morning appointments. I checked the book to see what was left for the day. It was Wednesday, one of my slower days. This gave some free time to sit back and focus on how to get some info on ole boy. Charley had knowledge of all the major players in the game, and I was pretty sure he was a dope boy. I could've asked Jazmine, the nail technician, but hell, nah! That bitch was known as the neighborhood slut bucket. I couldn't risk her trifling ass snatching him up for herself.

Charley finally decided to show his face. He gets on my last nerves, behaving like he got it like that, and he shows up whenever he wants to. I'ma bounce on his faggot ass as soon as I saved up enough money to get my own spot.

"What's poppin', Si'," Charley greeted me.

"Chillin'," I replied nonchalantly.

"Gurl, my bad! I was out with the fellas all night, gettin' our party on. You know how we do."

"Yea, whatever!" I rolled my eyes at him. He saw his excuse wasn't sitting well with me, so he walked off to greet one of his customers.

I waited patiently until he was finished; then I walked over to him. "Aye, Charley."

"Whaddup, Si'?" he quizzed.

"I need to know the 4-1-1 on a dude name Alijah." I explained the whole fiasco that happened between Alijah and myself. I could tell by the expression on his face that he knew who I was talking about.

“Charley, listen, I’m feelin’ him and need to know who I’m fuckin’ wit’, and most important, is he paid?” I looked at him and bust out laughing, followed by my version of Kanye West’s song, “I ain’t saying I’m a gold digger, but I ain’t messin’ wit’ no broke nigga.”

Charley looked at me with disgust. “Sierra, money isn’t all to a relationship. You gon’ find a dude that’s gon’ turn yo’ young ass out; then you gon’ be up in here cryin’ the blues,” he warned sarcastically.

“Listen up, Charley! I ’on’t need no damn speech. Are you gonna find out or not? Save that bullshit for a bitch that cares.” *This nigga sure is acting like my daddy*, I thought.

He must’ve sensed the hostility in my voice ’cause he dropped the parental role real fast. “Yo, calm yo’ ass down,” he warned. “I know of dude,” he added.

I turned my full attention to him, not knowing what to expect. He started to spill the beans on ole boy.

“He’s a Jamaican dude from up top. He moved down here ’bout a year ago. He’s in charge of his crew . . .”

I took in everything he was saying, and when he was finished, I felt satisfied.

"Thank you, boo boo." I started to walk back to my stall when Charley grabbed my arm with a tight grip.

"Sierra, be careful. Word on the street, that nigga ain't nothin' nice to fuck wit'. You know how them foreigners gets down."

I snatched my arm away. "Thanks fo' the advice. And *I'm* nothin' nice to fuck wit'." I gave him a devilish grin and then sashayed off.

As I relaxed and waited on my next client to arrive, I could not help but wonder if God finally answered my prayer. I was proud of all the things I had accomplished, but my real plan was to find me a big-timer, get married, have a couple of kids, and move somewhere up in the hills.

I was shocked when Alijah showed up at my job. A visit from him was the last thing I expected, but I was thrilled. I noticed as he walked in, he became the focus of everyone's attention, which was filled with the neighborhood skeezers.

He asked me out for lunch, and I turned him down. I decided to play hard to get. I wasn't hungry anyway, and if he was really feeling me, he'd keep trying. He left with an attitude, but not before giving me his number.

Wow! He looked even better in the daytime. He had to be about six foot seven, dark, smooth skin with thick eyelashes, and a model build.

I decided to leave early. Charley had an attitude, but the last time I checked, I was grown as hell. I headed down Mechanicsville Turnpike, with no exact destination in mind. I just needed to clear my head. I was fortunate to have a ride—a 2004 Ford Taurus. I had to go through some bullshit just to get the car, but it paid off, though. Fair exchange wasn't no robbery. The dude, Tone, that owned the used car lot, sold it to me for the low-low in exchange for me going out with him. I ended up fucking him, which was a disaster because his dick was the size of a six-year-old little boy's. I wasn't tripping, but at least I had something to show for it.

Days went by, and I still hadn't heard from Alijah since the day I fronted on him. I must've lost out. I was tempted to dial his number but decided not to. I knew I was playing a dangerous game, but I had to test him. If he really wanted me, he wouldn't give up that easy.

My mood at work was fucked up too. I hadn't really said much to anyone except my clients. I thought about cancelling all my appointments for the week but decided against it. In reality, I needed the money. I was tired of living in the projects. The rent was cheap, and I was saving my money up. My goal was to open my own boutique. Charley wasn't going to keep pimping me. I wanted to be my own boss.

The day went by very slowly. *I could've stayed home*, I thought. Unfortunately, I didn't make that much. As usual, I was the last one to leave up outta there. It was still early. Spring was finally here, and the weather was beautiful. I wasn't trying to go home and sit in that boring-ass apartment. Sometimes I wish I had a roommate, a dog, or even a cat. I decided to hit the mall up and get me the new Jordans that had just dropped the day before.

I got the sneakers and headed on home. It was getting dark outside. I parked and checked my pocketbook for my .22. I nicknamed her Betty. I didn't go nowhere without her. I had seen my share of robberies and murders taking place after dark. I wasn't ready to fall victim to any of it.

I didn't get a chance to step in the door when my phone started to ring. I dropped the shoe box on the floor and dug into my pocketbook. I had too much junk up in there.

"Hello," I answered without looking at the caller ID.

It was Alijah. I could tell by his sultry voice.

I wanted to jump up and down, but instead, I held my composure. I was tired of beating around the bush, so I confessed and told him I was feeling him. I was ready to make him my man. We decided to hang out, so without hesitation, I gave him my address.

I didn't know what he had planned for the night. I decided to wear a black Ecko red strapless dress and Rocawear strap-up slippers to match. I tried to keep it simple. I had just got my hair braided in micros, so I pinned it up in a bun. I put a pair of cubic zirconia studs in my ear. Who knew what was going to happen, so I sprayed all over with Curve fragrance. There's an old saying, "Stiff dicks have no conscience."

My nerves were torn up. I kept pacing back and forth until I heard a knock on the door. I popped the door opened. I knew he was a stranger to my hood, and the niggas around there don't like to have others snooping around. I wouldn't know how to deal with it if anything was to happen to him while he was coming to see me.

Damn, this dude look good as hell, I thought. I wanted to pull him in and tongue him down. I caught him staring with his mouth wide open. I cleared my throat to let him know I was still standing there. He gave me a seductive look and licked his juicy lips just like LL Cool J would've done. I was pretty sure that my drawers were flooding with pussy juice by then. I didn't have time to check.

I closed the door and headed toward his car. While we were walking, I sensed uneasiness. I turned my head and saw exactly what the problem was. Li'l Tony and his flunkies were posted up. I put my arm around Alijah's waist so he could loosen up a little. We got to the car without any drama kicking off.

He took me to a Caribbean restaurant on the South Side. As we entered, I realized it was more elegant than the places that I had been to before. The setting was romantic. The only light that illuminated the dining room was that of scented candles.

The service was on point too. Alijah ordered curry goat and rice and beans. I decided to stick with the bird. I wasn't into eating all that crazy-ass food they be eating. Fifteen minutes later, we were grubbing as if we were starving. Any other time, I'd be shy to eat around a dude, but not him. I felt at ease, like I had known him for a lifetime.

I really enjoyed our first date. *A thug with a romantic side,* I thought as I lay back in the car seat. I looked over at him. He seemed like his attention was focused elsewhere. I knew if I wanted him to be my man, I'd have to step my game up. I'd been with a lot of dudes before him, but Alijah was different; he's a take-control type of dude. I would have to play my cards right.

Without even thinking about it, I reached over and grabbed his crotch. I looked at him to see his reaction. He seemed shocked! It was at that very second, I wondered if I made a mistake, but it was too late to get all scared, though. I was at the point of no return.

"Whaddup, ma?" he asked with a confused look on his face.

I didn't answer him. Instead, I gave him that "I wanna fuck you" look. I started to rub on his dick. I felt it rise up like self-rising flour in a frying pan. My pussy was paying full attention too. My clit was throbbing in my Victoria's Secret thong. I pulled his zipper open and released his cock. In front of me was the biggest, most beautiful cock that I had ever laid eyes on. I slowly reached over and licked the tip of it. I tried to be as gentle as I could. I had to keep in mind that he was behind the wheel.

I would've done anything to see the look on his face, but I was too busy trying to give his dick the attention that it yearned for. I tried to devour the dick, but I felt like I was about to throw up. Damn, it was huge, but being the pro I was, I started to deep throat it as if my life depended on it to survive.

I figured he couldn't concentrate 'cause he pulled over. In no time, his hands were between my legs. I was feeling hot and horny; my pussy was on fire. I just wanted to jump all over him. Plain and simple, I just wanted to fuck, but not yet. This was just a teaser to let him know what was in store for him if he played his position.

His dick got extra hard, so I knew he was about to bust. When I eased up off him, his energy juice gushed out. I wanted to open my mouth and secure every last drop but decided not to. I didn't want to come off as no slut. I came right along with him. I felt the sticky substance on my dress since my thong couldn't hold all my pussy juice.

I watched as he wiped himself off, then hand me some Kleenex. I put it between my legs and patted my cat down. When we were done, he pulled off and continued on as if nothing happened. I would have given anything to find out what was going on in his head. I hoped he wouldn't look at me differently. I usually didn't get down like that, but I saw something that I wanted, and I was going to get mines by any means necessary.

As he pulled up in front of my building, I felt sad. I didn't want the night to end, but I was at a loss for words.

"Bye," I said, opening the door.

Alijah grabbed my arm. "Ma, that's all you gon' say, 'bye'?"

I looked at him and shrugged my shoulders. I was speechless.

"Ma, I'm diggin' yo' style, and I'm tryin'a see what's really good wit' you; real talk."

"I like you too, Alijah. Let's see where our feelings take us."

"A'ight, that's whassup! Good night, sweetheart." He reached over and kissed me on the cheek.

"Good night. I'll call you," I said, exiting the car.

As I walked to my building, I noticed all eyes were on me. I felt what Tupac, the rapper, was talking about. I took a look at the scenario that surrounded me. There were some hood buggers hanging out on the steps; then there were the old heads who sat out there in the same spot from sunup to sundown playing cards and talking shit, and let's not forget the crackheads and the dopeheads. These were their favorite hours. I shook my head in disgust. I couldn't wait for the day to move out of the slum that I called home.

Alijah Jackson

Ever since I left the shop last night, I was in the zone. I didn't like the effect shorty had on me. I had dealt with all types of broads before, but she ain't like no other. She seemed independent, which was a plus because I didn't like fuckin' wit' no dizzy bitch.

I was tired of the suspense, so I jumped in my money-green Lexus GS 300—my favorite ride. I usually don't drive around town in it, but today, I was on a mission. I drove over to the West End to handle some business, then breezed through Jackson Ward to holla at my homeboy. I didn't like going through the Ward like that 'cause jakes was always posted, like a fiend waiting to cop their drug of choice. I had been careful thus far to avoid being on their radar. I planned to keep it that way because I've heard plenty stories about the federally in Virginia.

My stomach was growling, so I decided to go see if shorty wanted to join me. I parked at the corner of the building and checked my burner. When I walked up in the crowded shop, I spotted her right away. She was doing some dude hair. I tried to read her expression, but she didn't let on. I felt all eyes on me, so I played it cool. I wasn't goin' to get played in front of all these cats.

"Whaddup, ma, I come through to see if you wanna join me for lunch."

She busted out laughing. "Do I look hungry or something?" she snickered.

"Nah, it ain't that. I felt like we started off on the wrong foot, yameen? Just wanna make up."

"Just finished eatin', plus I'm busy."

"A'ight, that's cool. Take my digits and get at a nigga when you not busy."

I got into the car. I had to sit down for a minute before pulling off. I was tight as fuck that I just got played by a bitch. I smacked the steering wheel to release frustration, then pulled off and sparked me a blunt.

My attitude was on one thousand. I wasn't in the mood to be around anyone. Instead, I decided to go to the Telly on Midlothian Turnpike, but before doing that, I called my bitch Luscious. Then I went and bought me a six-pack of Guinness and a pack of Dutch. My intention was to get fucked up and get fucked.

Time waits on no one, so I returned my focus on what I knew best. I couldn't let pussy get in the way of my hustle. There's plenty of bitches tryin'a get at the kid. I had a feeling that she was digging me, but instead, she insisted on playing her little-ass games. She had the game fucked up. I wasn't into chasing bitches. I get pussy thrown at me on the regular. She would realize soon enough that she was missing out on nine-and-a-half inches of the best wood in town.

I made a few stops, then headed out to Henrico County. The guys were waiting on me. Business was crazy for a few days; my money kept coming up short. I had Markus going over the count a couple of times before I called the meeting, and he assured me it was still the same.

As I drove, all different scenarios ran through my head. *It better be a good fuckin' reason why my shit keeps comin' up short*, I thought.

I strongly believed in loyalty and would hate for one of my niggas to be the culprit. Death was the only solution I knew when it came down to disloyalty. Mmm . . . I hope I was tripping for niggas' sake.

The block was quiet, as usual. I scoped out my surroundings before I pulled into the back. Everything seemed straight. I checked my waist. Even though those were my family inside, I still came prepared, and money is the root of all evil. I entered without warning. Niggas' voices could be heard blasting from the living room. When I entered the room, everyone's attention turned to me.

"What's up, fellas?" I gave dap to each of them.

"Whaddup, Boss?" they replied in unison.

I sat across from Darryl. I wasted no time on small talk. I started to spit out what I had to say, the whole time gritting on them. They started to throw blame elsewhere, mostly on the runners. No one wanted to man up and take responsibility.

"Yo! Yo!" I said to end the bullshit.

"Listen, y'all, I 'on't kno' who fuck wit' mi bumbo claat money, but bottom line is somebody gon' pay wid dem fuckin' life. Dats mi rass word." I paused for a second, then continued. "I can't say fo' sure who the pussy claat culprit is, but I can't have no rass claat snake pon mi team. So, yes, you *are* yo' brotha keeper when it cum dung to my bread."

"Yo, son, what the fuck you mean by that?" Darryl lashed out.

"Brethren, no disrespect, but you know how I feel 'bout mi money. Niggas is tryin'a disrespect me."

"Yo, Marcus, I want you to pay full attention. From now on, count the bags in front of dem. That way, a nigga can't claim it was all there, and y'all do the same wit' y'all workers." I looked directly at Chuck and Dre.

Then I got up and walked out without any response, slamming the door behind me. I'm pretty sure that niggas got a clear picture that I wasn't playing around. I knew Darryl was feelin' some type of way, but I wasn't gon' back down. I knew he wasn't no punk either, but at this point, it's whatever. I needed to know that I could trust the people around me. If I had to question their loyalty, then who the fuck could I trust? No one . . .

I was beat as hell. Whoever said hustling was easy told a damn lie. I couldn't complain because I came from nothing to having a couple of pieces of real estate, expensive rides, and more money than I could ever spend in this lifetime.

It surprised me that shorty didn't get back with me. She had managed to do what no other bitch had been able to do—captivate my mind. I'ma punish the pussy when I finally lay hands on her. I pulled my phone out and dialed her number. The phone rang a couple of times before she picked it up. I was shocked that she wasn't on no bullshit. She had finally come to her senses, and we decided to kick it for the night. I hung up and headed on home to get dressed.

I wanted to impress her. I put on a pair of dark indigo jeans by DKNY with a Sean John shirt to match and a fresh pair of Jays. I kept the jewelry simple; didn't want to attract unnecessary attention.

I made a quick turn on Q Street; then I headed to Creighton Court Projects. The apartment number was visible because I wasn't going to waste my time searching. I checked my waist; I had to make sure that my burner was in place. I didn't like being in the projects in the daytime, much less at the night.

I approached her building with caution. A few cats were standing by the corner. I kept eye contact until I passed them; all along I kept my hand on my nine. I was also on the lookout for jakes; they were known to be patrolling on dirt bikes or just walking around.

She opened the door on the first knock, which was a point for her. I didn't want to linger out in the open. I was stunned when I noticed just how radiant she looked. She was in a skintight dress. My mouth popped opened as if I was in a trance, and she caught me staring.

"Hellooooooooo, I'm right here!"

I really enjoyed dinner with her. The night was about to end, and I didn't want it to. I wanted to take her to the Telly and fuck the shit out of her but decided to take it slow for once. I was really digging her style. We hadn't said much of anything to each other since we left the restaurant. I met plenty of bitches who wouldn't shut up for a second, but she was laid-back, listening to the *Carter 11* CD.

I was shocked when I felt her hand on my dick. I felt like I wanted to bust outta my pants. She then leaned over and started to give me some good-ass head. It didn't take long for me to bust. I totally forgot that I was in public. I pulled some napkins out and wiped my hand off before pulling off. I didn't want the night to end, but I was cool for the moment. I made a mental note that I was going to cuff her. The rest of the ride was on quiet mode. I think we were both lost in our thoughts.

When I pulled up by her complex, she tried to leap out of the car, so I grabbed her and sat her ass down. I let her know what my intention with her was. I wasn't into playing little kiddie games. After I got that out of the way, I kissed her on the cheek. I had certain rules 'bout kissing on females. She got out. I waited until she got in her building; then I pulled off. I was exhausted, so I headed home.

Chapter Four

Shayna Jackson

I'm the *bitch* that rewrote the meaning of *high definition*. I'm intelligent, independent, and sexy. I was born and raised in Hempstead, Long Island. My parents were prominent civil case lawyers in NY.

I was exposed to the good life from birth, so it's only right that I continued on into my adult life. I was molded to be someone of importance, from living in a gated community to playing the piano, and then later, ballet classes to gymnastics. You name it, and I've done it. I had all the finer things money could buy. Being an only child only helped the situation.

I graduated from high school at the top of my class. I then went on to college, then law school. Now I was a top-of-the-line defense attorney. I was the head bitch in charge!

I learned early on, everyone came with a price in life. So whether it's opening my legs or getting on my knees, I made sure the judges that presided over the cases I represented were well taken care of. Truth be told, it's well worth it. Everyone was content in the end. The judges got a taste of some of the best-bred pussy they ever had in their lives, the drug dealers got little or no time, and me, I got a fat-ass account at Bank of America.

Every man I knew wanted a chick like me to call wifey. Who could blame them? I'm five foot eight, dark chocolate, with a straight face and slanted eyes. I had a body like a model. My long, coal-black hair reached all the way down my ass. I'd say I favored Naomi Campbell. I was all natural. Money could buy you beauty, but you had to inherit class.

I met my husband Alijah in February of 2002 at a Valentine's Day party that one of my clients was hosting. It was love at first sight, or so I thought. From the moment that I laid eyes on him, I just knew I had to have him. He was a tall, handsome brotha; the type that make you stop dead in your track and say, "Damn, who is that."

The way he was dressed, I could tell he was a major player in the illegal world. Nevertheless, I was attracted to him. There was something about thugs that gave me a rush. Their in-control attitude really did something to a sister.

On my way out the door, I slipped him my business card, and within a few days, he called me. I knew he wasn't locked up, so it wasn't business; it was personal. We went out for drinks all the way on the Upper East Side in one of Manhattan's elite bars.

Alcohol and a sexy woman can sure alter a man's persona. It didn't take long for Alijah to start bragging about who he was and how well connected he was. My type of dude. A thug with long pockets. His destiny was controlled after that night without him even knowing it.

After a couple of months of wining and dining at upscale restaurants, weekends in the Poconos, and trips to Jamaica, my ass got pregnant; then he proposed to me. He almost blinded me when he popped out the 4.5-carat diamond ring. That's what I was talking about; a man that didn't care about how much he spent on me. After all, I gave good head and ride a helluva dick.

Don't be fooled by this good-girl persona. I knew how to get what I wanted in life, so playing the submissive wife was easy. Whatever my husband wanted, he got. However, the honeymoon was over before it started. It didn't take long for him to show his real color.

At first, I wouldn't feed into the bullshit. He's a major player, so at first, I didn't fuss when he was never at home . . . I gave him an inch; he took a whole fucking yard. I would call his phone, and it would be turned off. See, Mama didn't raise no fool. A drug dealer only cuts their phone off when they didn't want to be found.

He had the money, good looks, and nine inches of a woman's wish. With that, all these project-living, loudmouthed, weave-wearing bitches came a dime a dozen, trying to get their measly hands on my husband in hopes that he was going to take care of them and their badass kids and move them out of the projects. Over my dead body was that going to happen. Them hoes would get nada but a wet ass and nightmares.

I kept tabs on his money, but he was smarter than I thought. Even though we had a joint account, I later found out that he had a personal one. I had to figure a way to get into that account too. It was easier than I thought. My husband's accountant, Markus, was no different than the men that I've dealt with before. He was weak, so I played on him with my sex appeal. It was scary at first because I didn't know how he was going to react or how loyal he was to Alijah and that would've been a death sentence.

It had been two years since we started our rendezvous behind Alijah's back. I couldn't front; he gave some good head, but his dick game was as weak as a severe case of anemia. He should've been ashamed to whip that little-ass dick out in front of a dame like myself. Another place, another time. If I were another bitch, I possibly could see a future between us. However, as of the moment, his money was chump change when compared to my husband's money. Plus, he wasn't no gangsta.

Lately, he made me nervous talking about he was in love with me. I had to bust out laughing when he told me that crap. For me, it was strictly business, nothing personal, and I could tell he was serious by the look on his face. If I didn't know how scared he was, I'd consider him a liability.

I fell out of love with Alijah a long time ago, but I damn sure loved his money. When he told me we had to move to Virginia, I quickly agreed. It was time for a change. I was running out of judges to blackmail, and I couldn't risk some ass prosecutor catching on to my scheme. That would be an embarrassment I couldn't endure. I couldn't jeopardize my relationship with my parents, either. It was already strained because I didn't marry a corporate husband. They'd definitely disown me, and getting cut out Daddy's will was not what I had in mind. The more money, the happier I would be.

I was glad to move elsewhere. Alijah had been fucking everything with a pussy. He thought that I wasn't aware of all his affairs with all the different women, but Markus's mouth be having a severe case of diarrhea. After sex, he spared no details of all the dirt that Alijah was dishing out.

The house we bought was beautiful; it reminded me of one of those old Victorian houses. By the time I put my final touch of decorations and purchased the finest furniture money could've bought, it was nothing short of a palace for a queen like me.

We lived in a boring-ass town a little outside of Richmond, but I could adapt to whatever situation as long as it involved the dead presidents. If I thought the move would bring us closer, I was wrong; it was a new saga about to start.

Chapter Five

Sierra Rogers

Me and my boo became inseparable. He'd pick me up after work, and we'd hang out. We would hit the croaker spot over on Jefferson Davis Highway and get us some steamed crab legs or to the Jamaican spot for some jerk chicken. After that, we'd go to the crib and smoke blunt after blunt of some high-grade herb.

My feelings were getting stronger by the minute. I ended up giving him some of this bomb-ass pussy on the third date. I was pleased by this man because he was a pro at eating pussy. He ate me up as if I were his last supper; then he laid the dick game down. I was hurting for days, but I loved it and wanted it on the regular. I knew I blew his mind after performing my dick-pleasing skills, and then rode him from the back, all along in my mind singing a verse out of

Lil' Kim's, "*I used to be scared of the dick, now I throw lips to the shit, handle it like a real bitch.*"

It was Thursday night, and we were kicking it. I wasn't feeling him coming over because I could tell niggas were already hating on him by the stares they gave us when we walked by. I was no fool. I knew it was a matter of time before one of them would approach me. I wasn't going to sit around and watch them fuck up my only chance of getting out of the projects. He wasn't flashing his money, but seeing is believing, and anyone with good eyesight could see money from a mile away.

I wanted to warn him of possible danger but didn't want to scare him off. I'd let him know soon enough, though. By then, I should be out of the hood and living more upper class.

A lot had changed between us, including me opening up a little more in conversations. So far, everything about him seemed right, even though I sensed there was someone else in his life. I was nervous about asking him, due to the fear of the answer I might get. I really didn't give a rat shit because a new sheriff was in town (me), and I was running *this* show.

I learned that he was from Jamaica, but grew up in New York. He was an only child like me. I sensed he was close to his mom, the way he talked about her with pride. It made me a bit envious because I lost mines to the streets. I hated to speak of her, but deep down, I wished she had chosen me instead of the streets.

Tears welled up in my eyes. That's a topic I was never able to handle. One day, I was going to see a shrink that could explain to me why that bitch chose a glass dick over her own flesh and blood, but for now, that bitch was dead in my eyes.

I quickly wiped my tears and snapped back to reality. I gave him a fake smile to assure him everything was cool. I didn't want to give the impression that I was a weak bitch. As I lay in his arms feeling protected, I wondered how long it will last. My plan was to hang on for dear life.

Sierra Rogers

Life was good. I went from wearing Rocawear and Baby Phat to wearing Gucci and Prada. He certainly knew how to spoil a girl because my closet was full of the latest designer clothes and shoes. I had finally hit the jackpot and was working my way up the ladder. The power of the P-U-S-S-Y! My next move was to upgrade to a classier ride and a condo on the James River.

The weekend was here, and I was bored out of my mind. Alijah was out of town. I wished he had taken me with him, but he had to go handle business. I didn't want him to think I was one of those codependent bitches, so I decided to chill until he got back.

I hadn't been out lately either since we started kicking it. I had been neglecting my best friend, Neisha. We've been friends for as long as I could remember. Up until high school, we were inseparable; she was my partner in crime. We kind of grew apart in our adult years. I enrolled in beauty school while she went for nursing at VCU. We still talked on the phone from time to time, and I still hooked her hair up.

I dialed her number.

"Hellooooooooo," she answered.

Gosh, I hated when she dragged her words. She reminded me of Sheneneh on *The Martin Lawrence Show*.

"What's up, bitch?" I asked.

"Bitch, I ain't heard from yo' ass in over a month," she commented.

"I know, just been busy workin' and tryin'a move," I lied. I really hate to lie to my girl like that, but I wasn't ready to tell her about me and Alijah. Plus, she asked too many damn questions.

"I'm bored. Let's hit Bojangles up. You know it's Sunday; it's on and poppin'."

"You paying 'cause I'm dead-ass broke? Just paid my rent and bought some books."

"Yup, I gotcha. Don't I always?" I asked with annoyance. "Bitch, just be ready. I'ma pick you up at ten o'clock," I said, then hung up the phone.

Dang! I loved Neisha, but this bitch kills me. She have all those lame-ass niggas digging her gut out, and still her pocket stays on empty. She needed to learn a thing or two from me, 'cause ain't anything for free, and pussy is high commodity. You see, Alijah ass already paying his dues.

My outfit for the night was a black, strapless Versace dress with a low cut in the back and a pair of black Steve Madden stilettos. I decided to wear my hair down and put on a minimum amount of Maybelline's foundation. I was a natural beauty, so I didn't have to put on no whole lot of makeup.

I glanced at myself in the mirror. My curves filled out every inch of the dress. I sprayed myself with White Diamonds fragrance.

***

I headed to the South Side. I sure wished Neisha lived closer. She needed her whip. I pulled up at the apartment complex that she shared with her two uppity white friends. I honked the horn, and she came out in a white one-piece, body banging as if she hit the gym on the regular, but I knew better. The only exercise that heifer did was sexercise.

"What sup, bitch?" she said as she entered the car.

"Nada, tryin'a get my grown and sexy on."

"I hear that. Can't wait to see what balla I'ma get these hands on tonight," she said, digging into her pocketbook.

"Look what I have here," she teased while dangling a fat blunt in the air.

"Yo, bitch, light that shit up so I can get right," I demanded.

"Calm yo' nerves, bitch. I got this."

She lit the blunt up and took a couple of drags before passing it to me. I took a long drag and started to cough. I tried to catch my breath.

"Bitch, you a'ight? Take yo' time, yo' greedy ass." She busted out laughing.

I took a few more drags, then passed it back to her. By the time I got downtown, I was high as a kite. I had to give credit to this heifer; she always managed to come up on some good smoke. Wished she was as lucky with her men.

As I pulled into the parking lot of the club, I peeped the line was ridiculously long. I glanced over at Neisha. She was high as a bitch.

"Gurl, let's get our party on." I found a space toward the back door. By the looks of things, it seemed to me all the money niggas were in there. The parking lot was full of Hummers, Escalades, Bimmers, and Benzes; it would be the police's dream to stop by.

The music was on point. They played a little bit of everything, and they kept announcing that Beenie Man was going to be in the house. I usually don't like dudes with dreads, but he was one sexy muthafucker who could get it at anytime.

I noticed all the island girls showing off their skills on the dance floor. I had to give it to them; they were doing the damn thing. When Sean Paul's "Gimme the Light" came on, I couldn't control my urge any longer.

I started to wind my waistline. The guys started to cheer me on while the bitches tried to step up, but I didn't let up. Somebody should've warned them. I got on my hands and flipped my body upside down and started to Tic Tac, and then shook my moneymaker with a vengeance. That alone shut those hoes down. The niggas were pleased. After the song ended, I flipped back on my feet and straightened my clothes while the selector kept shouting me out.

"Bitch, you did that," Neisha said, slurring her words.

After the performance, I was tired as hell. I must've forgotten that I wasn't sixteen anymore. My feet were hurting from the six-inch heels I was wearing. Neisha ass done disappeared on me. Knowing her, she might've been up in the bathroom fucking or something. I needed another drink, so I made my way to the bar. *This is going to be my last drink for the night*, I thought. This would turn out to be so damn true!

I made my way to the bar and got me a glass of Hpnotiq. On the way back to my table, I was stopped dead in my tracks. I blinked a few times to make sure the alcohol didn't have me bugging out. The images were still there—clear as a brand-new mirror!

Alijah Jackson, my man, my nigga, or whatever you chose to call him at the moment, was standing in front of me in living color *kissing another bitch*. I hesitated for a minute so I could regroup. *What the hell*, I thought. *I'm his woman.*

I strutted my black ass over to where they were standing and tapped him on the shoulder, interrupting their little make out sessions. "Excuse me," I said, clearing my throat.

Both of them turned around to face me. I kept my eyes focused on Alijah. I knew his expression was going to be worth a million bucks. He looked at me as if he had just seen a ghost.

"Whaddup?" this nigga asked as if I was bothering him.

"You," I replied with venom in my voice and a deadly grin on my face.

"What's going on, Alijah. Who is this woman?" This bitch spoke up with a look of confusion on her face.

"Well, hello, I'm Sierra, but you can call me Si'; that's what Alijah call me," I stated.

I stretched my hand out for a handshake, but the bitch didn't respond. She placed her hand behind her back.

"So, Alijah, the cat got yo' tongue? Are you going to introduce me to this lovely young lady?" If looks could kill, I would've been one dead bitch. "Well, since he won't introduce me, I'm Shayna, Alijah's *wife,*" she spoke in perfect English, then stretched out her hand to display the huge rock she was wearing on her finger.

I wondered if I heard the bitch right. This son of a bitch was married. "Oh, nice to have finally met you. Alijah told me such nice things about you," I straight up lied. Why I did that, I have no clue. "Haven't you, Alijah?" I asked with a devilish grin.

"It's nice to meet you, but I have to go find my fiancé. He should be wondering where I'm at by now."

Alijah's eyes popped opened; that gave me a sense of gratification. I said good-bye, then sashayed off.

My heart had just got ripped into a million pieces. My eyes began to gather water, but I used my might not to further humiliate myself. I looked around for Neisha; she was nowhere to be found. I bumped into a little nigga we knew, and he told me she left with Big Earl, a big-timer from Fairfield. I cussed under my breath and walked off.

As I sped down Broad Street, I was crying my heart out. I didn't give a damn if police were out. I jumped into a parking space that I wasn't sure belonged to me. The effect of the alcohol was taking its toll on me. I fumbled around in my pocketbook and found the keys to the apartment. After failing numerous times to find the keyhole, I finally got the door open and fell head on in.

The next day came and almost left without me knowing. I woke up around six in the evening. I had a really bad headache from all the alcohol I drank the night before. I should've never got fucked up, but it was too late for regrets.

I took a shower and downed two Tylenol PM to cure my headache, but I was going to need something stronger to cure my broken heart. I jumped up and threw some sweats on with a wife beater and flip-flops and ran upstairs to Li'l Jon Jon's apartment. He stayed with some good smoke. I copped a twenty bag of Arizona and headed downstairs.

I rolled me a fat blunt and lay back on the sofa. Then I started to replay the whole scene in my head and started bawling again, only this time harder.

"Damn you, Alijah! How could you do this to me?" I asked retroactively.

I threw the glass of orange juice that I was drinking at the wall. Broken glass shattered everywhere as juice dripped down the wall. That's exactly how my heart felt at the moment.

When the smoke illuminated my brain, I felt like a brand-new woman. My tears were dried up. My pain was turned into anger. "Wife," I kept repeating to myself. This nigga played me for a fool. He wasn't shit but a two-timing asshole. I wondered how I could be that blind.

A rush of jealousy came over me. This bitch didn't even look like the average broad. I tried to find out her fault. When I inspected her from head to toe, not a piece of hair was out of place, and I could tell she shopped at the finest stores.

I couldn't clown her ass even if I wanted to, and that rock on her finger made her shine even more.

I noticed my cell hadn't rung at all since I had been awake. I took it out and saw that it was dead. I plugged it up and checked my messages.

"*You have no new messages at this time. Press three to check old messages,*" the operator said on my T-Mobile phone. I closed the phone, feeling disappointed. I was really hoping he'd call. Even though I was mad as hell, he could've at least apologized.

All kind of scenarios ran through my mind; what was he doing, and was he with her while I was here by myself? I put in a Mariah Carey CD and switched to my favorite song, "Shake It Off." Her words didn't help none because I couldn't shake the feeling. This nigga had my heart in the palm of his hands. That's when something hit me. I remembered when we first started kicking it. I had a feeling that someone else was in his life. I was too scared to ask, and he didn't volunteer the information.

Alijah Jackson

The phrase "money ova bitches" has always been my motto, but I definitely was slacking on my paper chasing. I was putting in overtime when it came down to spending time with shorty.

I already knew her head game was on one thousand, but I was curious about the punany. I wasted no time letting her know I wanted to fuck. I laid the pipe down like a real nigga should. She took it like a beast. Every stroke I threw, she threw that ass back. I fell in love when I flipped her on her back and started to long dick that pussy. The pussy was so fucking good I busted quicker than usual. If I wasn't careful, she might become suicidal over the dick. That thought blew my mind.

My next move was to take her out of the hood. I wasn't feeling that place. I had a weird feeling whenever I pulled up over there. I felt like niggas were plotting on me. They had reputations for being Jock Boys. They don't show you no love, especially if you're not one of them. I knew I was treading on thin ice. This was her home team, and I believed if she heard anything, she'd holler at me about it. An old head once told me, "Never put your trust in anyone, especially a woman." I figured I should listen.

It had been days since I handled any form of business. I let Darryl know my whereabouts, but other than that, I was chilling.

I told her what I did for a living, but I didn't get too much in my personal life. We rapped about our lives growing up. I learned that she experienced a tough life growing up. I felt she had some issues she wasn't telling me about. A felt tear dropped from her eyes, and I pulled her closer to me so she would know that those days were over. I got this.

I also spent a lot of bread on her too. We'd hit the mall up almost every day. I'd spend a couple of Gs on clothes, shoes, whatever her heart desired. She was my bitch, so she had to represent.

The weekend was finally here. After a stressful week, a shipment came in from up top, so we got together and broke it down. The streets were dry, and niggas were hungry; therefore, every second wasted meant a missed chance to make more paper. Now that things were straight, I could sit back and collect my paper. I was a millionaire. Who'd ever guessed that a li'l runny-nosed dude from the gutter would've been the HNIC of those streets?

I pondered how long it would last. Word in the street was that niggas wasn't feeling us making money out there. It was expected, though, 'cause Mosby and Creighton niggas thought they were untouchable. I had to give it to them li'l niggas; they had heart. I was gon' let them get their shine on, and in due time, I was going to shut them down.

I almost felt some type of fucked-up vibes coming from my nigga too. Ever since the other day when we had words, Darryl seemed distant. Although we squashed the shit, and he said everything was cool, my instinct told me different. Dude was my brother, so if he said it was, then, that's what it was.

It was Sunday night, and we usually were up in the Canal Club down in Shockoe Bottom. It be jumping with honeys. Plus, if you wanted to take in some good reggae tunes, it was the place to be. Tonight, the doctor was blowing up in Bojangles, another Jamaican spot, so I hit Darryl up.

"Yo, whaddup, son?" he answered.

"The doctor is 'bout to be up in Bojangles tonight."

"That sound like a plan, yea, 'cause I need some fresh pussy," he bragged.

I didn't comment because he's my boy, but he changed bitches more than his drawers. But that's my ace, so whatever floats his boat.

"A'ight, son, that's what is."

"One." I hung up.

I took a shower and got dressed. As I headed out the door with a sexy looking female by my side, I was ready to get my party on.

A rush of guilt swept on me as I drove down Broad Street. I hate the fact that I had to lie to Sierra. I had her believing that I was outta town. Fuck it, I can't let her know my every move. I do a lot of dirt and couldn't afford to get torn off. I also needed a chance to breathe.

I parked my car in the space closest to the exit. I checked and made sure my burner was loaded before getting out. Security was tight as usual, but I had my homie waiting at the door.

I stepped out of my cream-colored Benz—my choice of ride for the night—with a badass chick by my side. I felt like the King of the South the way I was flossing. I walked by a few bitches that tried to holla at me, but now wasn't the right time, so I kept it moving. I gave the bouncer five bills and kept on.

I immediately peeped my niggas. I gave them dap, and we headed to the VIP, where bottles of Dom P, Cristal, and Grey Goose with grape juice were waitin' on us. Darryl had 'bout a pound of Haze and Dro; our intention was to get fucked up.

A couple of broads came back there with us, but I couldn't fuck around, though. I looked over at my company. She was still as beautiful as the day I met her. However, a lot had changed. My feelings were not the same, but we had been through so much, I was hesitant to say, "Fuck her."

The selector was on top of his game. He kept coming with some old-school reggae; nothing but the best. All hell broke loose when one of Sean Paul's songs came on. Bitches crowded the dance floor the same way cockroaches made their appearance when the lights go out in an infested apartment. There was this one chick that was doing the damn thing. Others tried to compete, but she shut them down. I tried to catch a glimpse of her face, but her back was toward me, and I didn't want to get caught peeping. I couldn't help but wonder where her man was while she was out acting a damn fool.

It was almost time for the doctor to hit the stage. I was ready for his performance. My cell started to vibrate. I had a feeling it was Sierra blowing me up. I decided to call her back later or something. I'll take her shopping, then dick her down, which will make up for my wrongs.

Right about now, I was high and tipsy. I felt like I wanted to fuck; instead, I was up in the club. Beenie Man better give his best, or I'ma ask for a refund.

Shorty was feeling her drinks too 'cause she started to rub on me. I tried to resist, but she was persistent. I didn't want to seem suspicious, so I gave in when she tried to kiss me. I was ready to leave.

I didn't get a chance to share my intention because I felt someone tap my shoulder. My first thought was it was one of my boys. I turned around . . . It'd be an understatement if I said I was shocked! Sierra was standing in front of me in living color. Man, what the fuck! Where did she come from? My mind was racing; I had to think fast.

I was busted, but like a true player, I held my composure. I remembered the three cs: calm, cool, and collected. I put my game face on and braced myself for the drama that was getting ready to kick off. Any other time, I could've lied my way outta any situation, but this time, it was up close and personal.

"Yo, whaddup?" I greeted her. I tried my best to downplay the seriousness of the situation. I *knew* the seriousness of it. I knew for sure that she was ready to go the fuck off. This was one time in my life that I wished I could've just disappeared off the face of the earth before shit hit the fan.

Shayna Jackson

It was Sunday night, and surprisingly, Alijah asked me out. I accepted with ease. It wasn't very often that he took me out with him these days. He usually went out with his entourage. I couldn't stand to be around them, and I let them know every chance I got. Markus put me on to game that they were telling Alijah not to trust me; which was too bad 'cause I wasn't going anywhere in the near future.

My outfit for the night was a Vera Wang black, strapless dress and a pair of Jimmy Choo pumps. I let my hair down and put on my Revlon hot red lipstick. I chose a pair of diamond dangling earrings that Alijah bought me.

I looked myself over in the mirror and was pleased with my appearance, so I headed downstairs. I could tell Alijah was pleased to see how beautiful I looked. He looked good his damn self. We walked out. In a stranger's eye, we would've seemed like the perfect couple.

Wherever we went, he had connections, so we didn't have to go through all the long lines. We headed straight to the VIP. I looked around to scope out the scenery. Females looked on with jealousy in their eyes; probably wishing that they were in my position. I stared back at them with a devilish grin on my face that read, "Too bad, *I'm* the chosen one."

The night turned out better than I imagined. Alijah's "friend" . . . ha-ha . . . that high-priced ho, deserved a standing ovation for her performance. I saw right through her ghetto ass. You should've seen the look on Alijah's face; it was *definitely* a Kodak moment. I had to give it to him; he had upgraded from the regular hood rat that he usually slept with. Being a lawyer helped me to smell the bullshit from a mile away. Every word that came out that bitch's mouth was a damn lie.

I almost busted out laughing. When that ho heard me say I was his wife, her eyes popped open like she just smoked some crack. I really rubbed it in when I shoved my big-ass diamond in her face.

Chapter Six

Sierra Rogers

Alijah had been calling nonstop for the past couple of days. I tried my hardest not to pick up the phone. Even though I was hurting, I didn't want him to think for a second that I was one of these dumb-ass bitches out here.

As much as I tried to stay away from Alijah, that didn't last long. I was missing him more and more, so after playing hide-and-seek for a week, I decided to pick up the phone. I was excited to hear his voice, but I read him his rights and didn't let up any. He listened quietly without interrupting me, not once. After I finished, I gave in and told him I was missing him.

We decided to meet up in an open area. Not that I was scared of him or anything, but you never know. When I pulled up, he was already waiting on the bench. I had on a pair of tight stretched jeans with a skintight tank top. He kept his eyes glued to me as I strolled toward him. *Yeah, he miss me*, I thought.

"Whaddup, ma," he greeted me and gave me a hug.

I leaned my head against his shoulder. He smelled masculine; I loved that about him—a strong, sexy man. His freaky self then cuffed my ass with his hands and pulled me closer to him. I'm not going to front; it felt good. He better stop before I fuck around and get a quickie on these benches.

We talked for about an hour. He kept apologizing for his actions, he told me the truth about his actions, and he told me the truth about his marriage. He's been married for four years, but he was not in love with her. I took in everything he said, and I might be a sucker for love, but I believed everything he told me.

We ended up going back to my apartment and talking some more. For some crazy reason, I broke down crying in front of the nigga. I shed more tears than Niagara Falls. He held me in his arms and kept wiping my tears. At that moment, I totally forgot those hours ago when I was fuming with anger.

Our bodies were in cahoots. We were both in need of some good loving, so we wasted no time. We fucked and sucked for hours. We rested, got back up, then got right back at it again. I forgave him the second the dick entered my pussy.

I made my mind up that I was going to fight for my man. She might be married to him on paper, but his heart belonged to me. I wasn't going to give up that easy. Everything in my life had always been a challenge; this was no different. I was going to get my man back. She could play wifey, take care of home, but I was his Bottom Bitch.

We ended up staying in for a couple of days. I called in sick even though Charles knew I was lying. Alijah called his boy to handle business. We had food, weed, and alcohol, but most important, we had each other's love. If this was a dream, I didn't want to wake up.

Alijah Jackson

"Son, I'm tellin' ya, I peeped that shit the other night. Yo' ass was busted, plain and simple," Darryl said, laughing.

"Mm . . . That's crazy though. Sierra was s'ppose to be at the crib sleepin'. I was shocked she was up in the club, especially Bojangles. Then did you see the way she was starin' Shayna's ass down as if she was ready to beat her the fuck down?" I responded.

"Nah, son! She was ready to fuck *you* up. Baby girl looked like Laila Ali. You better watch yo' ass."

"Nah, son, that bitch know better than to put her hands on me," I replied with cockiness.

"Yo' black ass was sweatin', ready to piss on yo' self. I thought I would've had to come over there and save yo' ass from distress," he continued with his antics.

I sure wished this nigga would shut the fuck up; instead, he kept on clowning.

"She a bad broad too. Where the hell you found her at? Shayna mental ass gon' kill you."

This time, Chuck and Dre joined in on the laughter. I was tight, but I wasn't gon' let them see that.

"Yo mi a bad man. Mi 'ave e'eryting unda control. Trust mi, I got dis, brethren," I said in my raw Jamaican accent that only comes out when I'm angry.

I finished shooting pool. What was supposed to be a guy's night out turned into me leaving. Any other time, clowning on each other was a'ight, but tonight, I wasn't feeling it.

"Yo, fellas, I'm out. I'ma holla."

"Word, son, it's like that?" Dre asked.

"That's what it is, bruh," I responded before I headed out the door.

It was fucked up how I handled my dawgs, but they were on joke mode, and I wasn't. I had a lot on my mind. Shayna's nagging ass was threatening to get a divorce, which wasn't a bad idea. I was ready for her ass to bounce up outta my life so I could live a little.

Sierra kept ignoring my calls. I even went to her job, but she managed to duck me. I needed some type of order with these bitches. They needed some act right, and *I* was the nigga, *not* the other way around.

It was Wednesday night, and I was bored out of my mind. I decided to head to a little spot over in the South. I could chill and relieve some stress in the process. I smoked a blunt before I pulled up to the Paper Moon Titty Bar. They had some of the baddest bitches from all races.

I walked through the door and headed straight for the bar where I ordered a bottle of Grey Goose with grape juice and went to my favorite spot in the back. I peeped that they had a full house. I had been in here a few times, and each time, it seemed like as soon as I walked in and the dancers saw me, a money machine sign went up in their mind.

I wasn't stutting them, though. I was here to see one person. I reminisced on how I met her a month ago. She was doing her thing while niggas were hollering at her from left to right. As she flashed a couple of them, I just sat back and enjoyed the show . . . until I saw her wink at me. I nodded my head to show I recognized her.

After the performance, we hooked up in the Champagne Room, a.k.a. the fucking room. Shorty was like that. I found out her name was Luscious. That name fit her just right and did me justice 'cause I left out of there a well-satisfied man.

A light-skinned chick was doing her thing. I threw a few dollars. Luscious was up next. She came out in a two-piece, pink maid costume. She put an extra twitch in her walk knowing she had me and all the guys paying full attention. My wood was on full alert. If she wasn't a high-priced ho, I'd take her away from all the other eyes and make her my personal ho, but I had enough on my plate. Plus, she seemed like the type of broad that would choose money over loyalty.

I waited patiently, taking in the other chicks that tried to top her performance.

"Papi, sorry I took so long," she said in her strong Puerto Rican accent. She gave me a peck on my cheek, then sat on my leg. Had she moved an inch closer, she'd have felt my wood wide awake.

"No problem, ma, you good. I'm pretty sure you 'bout to make it up to me," I said invitingly.

"You kno' it, Papi. Let's go!" She took my hand and led me toward the back room.

The other guys looked on with lust in their eyes. One of her homegirls yelled something in Spanish, and she giggled. I looked at her and thought she could get it too.

I walked out a satisfied man. My problems were now on the back burner. Shorty worked magic with her tongue. In return, I peeled her off a good piece of change. I really wished that I could wife her, but I already knew . . . can't turn a ho into a housewife.

Sierra's ass 'bout to get dismissed, kick rocks . . . straight like that. I was not going to sweat no broad. Bitches were lined up ready to take her spot. I'd been leaving her messages; still no response.

Shayna's ass was back on her shit, asking me all kinds of questions. This bitch seemed to forget that I was a grown-ass nigga. I'd been sleeping in the guest room at our house. At this point, I didn't give a fuck if she left; the fucking marriage didn't mean shit to me. To keep it one hundred, the only reason I married the bitch in the first place was 'cause she was carrying my seed at the time. Then right after the wedding, she had a miscarriage. I was sick after that. I had plans for my little nigga. She took it extra hard, so I felt obligated to be there for her ass since the doctors said it was due to stress. I felt a little guilty since, at the time, I was ripping and running the streets. She's been using that ever since, throwing it in my face every time we got into a fight.

The drama on the streets began. Niggas had been asking a lot of questions about who I was and who I rolled with. It didn't surprise me that my name was ringing bells in the street. I was incognito, though. I moved too fast for these country muthafuckas. They had one advantage; they knew the ins and outs of the city's dead ends. I had been considering getting a bulletproof vest. It's a fed's charge, but fuck it. I'd rather be judged by twelve than carried by six.

I was spending a lot more time with the Puerto Rican chick too. She knew how to treat a nigga, and she did tricks with her tongue that had a nigga's toes curling up. I never had a bitch before licking my ass crack and blowing in my asshole. I doubled her paper after that.

I had called Sierra's phone for the umpteenth time. I was missing her, and even though I tried to dismiss her, my heart was in this one. I saw me and her in the future. She was definitely wifey material; she just needed to stop tripping like that.

Ring! Ring! Ring!

"Hello," her seductive voice echoed through the phone.

"Yo, ma, it's me."

"So, what you want, Alijah? Shouldn't you be callin' yo' wifeee?" she replied sarcastically.

"Ma, I kno' you tight wit' a nigga right now, but gi' mi a chance to explain myself to you," I pleaded.

"There's only one side to this story. You're married, and I'm not the lucky bitch," she said in a serious tone.

"I feel you, ma, but I just wanna see you and talk. If you 'on't like what I'm spitting, then I'll leave you alone," I suggested.

After letting her see things my way, we decided to meet up at the park. I knew if I wanted her back, I would have to come correct. She wasn't a slouch, so any old saying wasn't gon' fly with her.

I had no doubt I was gon' get her back; how long it was gon' take, I didn't know.

Shayna Jackson

Alijah had been behaving strangely, like he didn't want to be bothered. When I tried to rub on him, he gave me the cold shoulder. I tried to find out about this bitch that he was fucking with, but I kept coming up short, and Markus ass didn't know who I was talking about. He never lied to me before, so I had no reason to doubt him.

The impression that I got was that this ho had some type of hold on him. I needed to find out what her story was. His slick ass must've kept her a secret because Markus never mentioned her, as much as he loved rubbing in whatever dirt Alijah did with the hope that I was going to leave Alijah for him. He was such a dreamer. I knew as long as I kept selling him dreams and kept him satisfied, I could always rely on him.

Our last visit at the motel, Markus was really shook up. When I asked him what the matter was, this weak-ass nigga told me, "Alijah found out his money was short and threatened to kill whoever was responsible." He was shaking like he got the chills. He continued to talk recklessly about "how I'm not touchin' his paper no mo'." It took me damn near two hours of sucking and riding his little pony to get him to finally see things my way again.

I knew we had to be extra careful. Knowing my husband, there are two things he don't play about—his mother and his money. I was scared for my damn self if he ever found out that I was cheating and stealing from him. He was capable of doing some serious damage. I knew it didn't make a difference that we had the same last name.

Everyone knew that the Jamaicans were not to be fucked with. On several occasions, I've overheard a couple of conversations with him and his boys when he ordered niggas to be killed. He also got his hands dirty a few times. Those two cousins that hung around were also dangerous. They sent chills all over my body whenever I got close to them.

I didn't know much longer I could put up with Alijah and his bad behavior. He was still acting crazy! I had to throw a tantrum just to get fucked, which was a waste of time and energy because he rushed and busted in about three minutes. I could've done better with Markus.

I've hated him ever since I lost my baby boy a year and a half ago. I was five months pregnant. This baby was going to be my prize to hold on to Alijah for life and secure me a permanent place in his pockets. Unfortunately, I had a miscarriage, and things haven't been the same since. My love for Alijah got buried with my son.

We got into another big fight, and he stormed out the door. I haven't heard from him since. I kept calling, but I kept getting voice mail. That's fine; two can play the game.

As soon as his truck pulled out of the driveway, I got on the phone and called Markus. His punk ass was against coming over to the house, but he came anyway. I took him straight to the bedroom, onto the bed I shared with my husband. Payback is a bitch!

I sucked the black off his dick and then straddled him. This one time, I could actually say that I enjoyed myself a little too much. After we were finished, I didn't bother to change the sheets.

Chapter Seven

Alijah Jackson

"*I'm the man in my city, ain't nobody fuckin' wit' me. You can ask the real niggas and all the bad bitches,*" T.I.'s voiced blared through the speakers of my brand-new, customized 2006 Range Rover. I had my eyes set on this ride for a minute. I love my Escalade, but I needed a change. I had them customize the interior with the Rastafarian colors: red, green, and black and put a lion covering on my seat to signify that I was the king of my throne.

I pulled up over to South Side Realtor in South Side Plaza. My man Walter worked over there.

"Whaddup, my man?" I greeted him.

"Alijah, it's a pleasure to see you," he said, getting up to give me dap. "What can I do for you?"

"I need to find a four-bedroom house or condo."

"What price range are we working with?"

"You know money ain't a thing," I replied with cockiness.

"All right, I might have something in mind. Let me check it out and get back with you."

"Sounds like a plan. Fax all the necessary papers over to my accountant. He'll handle it."

"I sure will," he said, sounding like he just hit the jackpot.

"Good lookin' out, Walt," I said before I left.

In a few days, Walter was on point. He found a house in a nice upscale neighborhood over in the West End. I met up with him, looked at it, and approved it. I wondered how Sierra would react. It was much nicer than the brick wall that she was living in at the moment.

I kept it a secret until everything was finalized. Walter set the paperwork up so it would be in Sierra's name. When you have money and power, you get shit done.

It was Labor Day weekend, and I was in New York. I headed to Mom-duke's crib. I hadn't seen her in a month. As I exited the New England Thruway onto Conner Street, I breathed a sigh of relief. It was always a good feeling whenever I went home.

As I cruised through the streets of Mount Vernon early in the morning, it was kind of chilly, so I slid my window down to let in some cool breeze. I looked around and ain't shit changed. Everything seemed the same. There was still a bodega on every corner; a Chinese restaurant and a Laundromat were within a mile radius. I couldn't help but notice that cats were still posted on the block waiting on that early-morning paper.

I parked on the side and walked up the driveway. When I knocked on the door, my mom opened it with a head full of pink and yellow rollers, as always.

"Hey, baby," she greeted me, opening her arms to give me one of her bear-type hugs.

"Hey, Ma." I bent down to plant a wet one on her cheek.

She was a little over four feet but had a voice that could cause an earthquake. We walked hand in hand into the house I bought for her two years ago. The aroma from her cooking filled the air. I knew we were goin' to be grubbin' in a little while. We rapped about everything, including family here and back in Jamaica. My uncle Johnny needed money again—for another "surgery." See, I didn't have a problem helping out family, but the problem with that was Uncle

Johnny wasn't really sick. The nigga had a coke problem, but knowing my moms and how naive she was, she was too blind to see that her favorite brother was a certified junkie.

We sat down and ate some fried dumplings, ackee, and codfish with hot cocoa. She knew how to throw down in the kitchen, and I sure missed her cooking.

I glanced over at her and saw a worried look on her face. Whenever she worried too much, it always took a toll on her health.

"Ma, is e'erything a'ight. You look sick or sump'n," I asked in a concerned tone.

"No, baby, I'm OK; tanks to do Jesus. It's you dat I'm worried about. You need to stop whatever you doin' before it's too late. Tek heed, mi bwoy; it's not good atall. You too damn hard head," she scolded.

I felt an uneasy feeling sweep over my body. I hated to see my mom hurting like that, but I wasn't ready to give up hustling.

"Ma, I'ma be a'ight. I just be chillin'," I lied.

"Alijah, a hard head make a soft ass." She looked at me with her coal-black eyes—eyes that made you think that she could see through your soul—She then got up from the table.

That was my cue that the conversation was over for now. As she began to clean up, I took the opportunity to step out on the porch and handle some business on the phone.

Later that night, I decided to head back to Virginia. It was always painful to leave my mom behind. Even though she was reluctant to take money from me, I always put a stack in her nightstand. As we hugged good-bye, I saw tears in her eyes. I wished that I didn't have to put her through these emotions, but reality was, a nigga gotta eat.

Thanks to the Almighty, I made it home safely. It was dangerous riding dirty on I-95. Many soldiers fell victim while taking that trip. You never knew what to expect, and that one trip might be your last trip.

Ring! Ring! My phone kept going off, so I checked my caller ID.

"Speak to me, son."

"Whaddup, bruh?" Darryl said, sounding agitated.

"What's it hittin' fo'?" I questioned, sounding concerned.

"Man, jakes ran up in the spot on Q Street early this mornin'."

"Word? Where you at?"

"I'm on Twenty-fifth Street 'cross from tha chicken spot."

My mind was racing; I tried to maintain my composure. I couldn't help but wonder how this happened.

Darryl was seated at a table when I walked in. I ordered me a Ginseng to throw off any suspicion of this meeting.

"Whaddup, son?" I gave him dap and sat across from him.

"One a tha workers called me 'bout four o'clock tellin' me tha spot just got hit. Luckily, no one was up in there at tha time. I got dressed and rushed ova there, and when I drove by, I saw Richmond's Task Force comin' out with garbage bags full of shit."

"What tha numbers?" I got straight to the point.

"They got 'bout half a key and ten stacks."

I clenched my teeth together and hit the table to show my frustration. "Yo, shut dat bumbo claat place down, and find out who a run dem pussy claat mout'. Jakes ain't dat fuckin' smart. Sum body mout' 'ave diarrhea, an' I wanna kno' who."

"I'm already on it. I'ma start with any nigga that got torn off recently. Also, I'ma check wit' my connect down at the station. She should kno' sump'n."

We sat for a little while longer, and then parted ways. As I headed out, a strange feeling swept over my body, like something wasn't right. Sometimes, I felt like I was being watched. Right then, I remembered the warning that Mom-dukes gave me a week ago.

I busted a U-turn and headed toward Fairfield Projects, where Saleem be at. He had called me a couple of days ago. I peeped his F-150 truck parked outside of his store. I couldn't help but think the brother was doin' it big. He had just opened this spot about three weeks ago. He sold everything from incense, oils, soap, and organic foods.

When I walked into the store, he was standing behind the counter. "Yo, my man, whaddup?" I greeted him.

"Peace, my brotha," he said and gave me pound.

"Let's sit down."

We walked to the rear of the store. He sat at his desk while I sat across from him.

"How's the business treatin' you?" he inquired.

"We eatin', but one of tha spots got hit by jakes this mornin'."

"Word! That's not good at all. That mean someone dropped a dime on the spot."

"Exactly, but also, lately, I've been feelin' like things ain't right. I've been havin' weird dreams 'bout getting locked up and wakin' up in cold sweat. I 'on't kno' what to make of all of this. That's why I'm here rappin' wit' you."

"Well, brotha, always remember to trust your gut instinct. When you're in tha game and gettin' the type of paper you're gettin', you gonna breed enemies from all angles." He paused, then continued. "You got niggas tryin'a get yo' spot in tha game, or the jakes tryin'a lock you up in the belly of the beast. Trust no one. Yo' best friend can become yo' worst enemy, brotha. Analyze yo' surroundings, and be yo' own eyes and ears. Leave it up to no one. You're yo' only keeper," he warned.

I sat there like a good student taking in all the knowledge that my mentor was spitting out.

"How is that wife of yours doing?" Saleem asked.

"Tha truth, son, haven't been home in days," I confessed.

"Well, keep an eye on her. A scorned woman can become a death sentence. Handle yo' business before it becomes a problem."

I walked out the door feelin' like I conquered the world. Saleem said something that hit the nerve. I wasn't close to a lot of people. I trust my niggas, and they proved their loyalty . . . so far.

As for the females that were in my life, I know Shayna bitches a lot, but she'd never do anything to hurt a nigga. I wasn't too sure 'bout Sierra, 'cause, even though she seemed loyal, I couldn't shake the feeling that she was one of them.

Sierra Rogers

I had been on my feet all day long. It was busier than usual. Summer was over, and all the little girls were getting ready to go back to school, so I had to hook them up with their little hairdos. I remembered when I was their age and wanted to look fly with my little updo.

My clientele was steadily growing, and I needed to get my own spot. There were four stylists and two barbers crammed up in a small-ass shop that you could barely move around in without bumping into each other. Charley didn't give a fuck as long as we were paying for our chairs. I wasn't feeling him anymore, but I felt obligated, because when I needed a break, he was there.

Ring! Ring!

"Hey, baby," I answered the phone, sounding too damn happy.

"You," he responded in a mischievous tone.

"Mm . . ." I chuckled. I felt like a high school girl all over again; shy, but yet feeling hot in the pants.

"Get ready. I'm comin' to scoop you up."

"Boy, you know I'm at work."

"I 'on't give a fuck. Tell that nigga you gotta go handle some business," he spoke with authority.

"Oh, what you have planned?"

"Don't worry 'bout all that," he spat.

"Dang! What's wit' the attitude. I was only playin' wit' you."

After picking me up, I noticed he was driving toward an upscale community over at the West End. Then he came to stop in front of a house. "Why are we parked here? Who lives over here?" I asked.

He didn't respond. Instead, he opened his door and got out. I was getting tired of his bullshit, so I opened my door and got out too. I was ready to give it to his ass, and I stormed toward him. Before I could even open my mouth, however, he handed me a set of keys.

"What are those for?" I shot him a stupid look.

"These are yours. Now go open the door to yo' house."

"House? Boy, stop playing wit' me like that."

"Shorty, go see fo' yo'self," he instructed me.

"Are you for real? Aah, aah." I jumped on him, hugging him.

He pushed me off him. "Go on, shorty."

I ran toward the front door. The whole time I was thinking if this was one of Alijah's sick jokes, I was going to kill him on the spot. I tried the first key, and it didn't work. I tried the second one—*bingo!* Oh my God! The first thing that I noticed was the hardwood floor, the shiny type you see on the infomercials on Saturday mornings.

I sped through the whole house in seconds; four bedrooms, wall-to-wall carpeting, the master bathroom was huge, and the kitchen was hooked up. I was so overjoyed I started to cry. I got on my knees and just wept. I finally had my own house.

I was into my emotions and didn't realize that Alijah was kneeling beside of me. I was aware of his presence when he wrapped his big arms around me.

"Thank you, baby, thank you," I said while hugging him.

"Ma, that's the least I could do fo' my woman." He helped me up from off the carpet and handed me a washcloth.

"*Sniff . . . sniff* . . . I'm grateful to you forever."

"Nah, you deserve this. Take it easy. Don't get all mushy on a nigga." He grabbed my arm. "C'mon, lemme show you the backyard."

"Wow! It's huge. I'm gonna need 'bout ten kids to play back here," I joked.

"Yo' ass crazy." He walked off, back into the house.

I followed behind him while he did his inspection. He stopped in the master bedroom and turned around to face me. "This where them ten babies gonna be made." He kissed my lips. I kissed him back passionately.

I leaned on his dick, which was pulsating on my throbbing pussy. I knew that I was ready to fuck. He was feeling the same way, so we went ahead and broke the new house in, butt-naked, on the hardest floor that I ever fucked on.

In my mind, it was well worth it. This man just bought me a house. The least I could've done was showed him my appreciation by slobbing on his knob and riding his cock. Life was lovely.

Chapter Eight

Sierra Rogers

It was the holiday, and my man was out of town, so I decided to go house shopping.

I called Neisha so we could hang out and catch up on each other's lives. I had been neglecting her since I started messing with Alijah. I picked her up, and we went to Value City Store. Word was that they had some nice-ass furniture for the low low. I found furniture for the entire house and made plans to have it delivered.

We weren't out of the store a good minute when Neisha started to interrogate me. "Bitch, where did you get all that money?"

"From my man—"

"Didn't know you have one of them," she spat.

I felt bad that I was holding out on my girl. I just wanted to keep my business out of the street for the time being. I went ahead and told her about him, from the incident at the club to him buying me a house.

"Bitch, a *house?* You lucky. What you had to do, suck his dick and lick his ass?"

"Yup that entire, plus swallow all his come," I bragged.

"Bitch, you scandalous, but you go, gurl. Get it while you can," she said, laughing.

I was glad that she was happy for me 'cause I loved Neisha to death. She was the closest to a family that I had. I dropped her off, but before she exited the car, I handed her $2,000. I knew she was struggling with her tuition and bills. Furthermore, if I was eating well, she was going to eat too.

The next day I went to the Housing Authority and told them I was leaving. I then went to Creighton so I could finish packing all those damn shoes I had. As I pulled up, I noticed Li'l Tony and the Creighton boys posted. They were known to run the projects, and they even had their signature "Creighton Boyz" tatted on their arms. I tried to slip by without being noticed, but it was too late.

"Sierra, what's poppin'?" Li'l Tony asked me while smiling, showing all thirty-two of his pearl-white teeth.

"Oh, hey, Tony." I really didn't care too much for him but didn't want to seem rude.

"You 'on't fuck wit' a nigga no mo'?"

"Boy, what you talkin' 'bout? I've been working, tryin'a to make some dough."

"Word, listen up. You're like a little sister to me, but you kno' the rules 'bout bringin' stray dogs home to eat without gettin' permission," he said with venom in his voice.

"Nah, you listen. I'm not yo' sister, so get to the fuckin' point." I folded my arms and gritted on him.

"Word in tha street is that you fuckin' wit' that dude from up top."

"Hmm . . . So what that got to do wit' you?"

He stepped closer to my face. I placed my hand on my pocketbook, just in case this nigga overstepped his boundaries.

"Yo, bitch, you one of us, right? So, you gon' help me set dude up 'cause I know he caked up. I'ma rob him, and I'll break bread wit' you."

I couldn't believe what I was hearing, so I took a couple of seconds to gather my thoughts. Then I spoke. "Nah, look, you charcoal-lookin' muthafucka. I'm not helpin' you do a muthafuckin' thing. You got the wrong bitch. Now get tha fuck outta my face before I spit on you!"

"Yo, bitch, who the fuck you talkin' to? I'ma get at ole boy one way or another, and if you stand in my way, I'ma split yo' wig too." He walked off with his flunkies not far behind.

"Fuck you, Anthony Smith. Yea, nigga, I know yo' government. Fuck wit' me," I yelled out in anger, then stormed off to my apartment. This nigga got under my skin. My next move was to upgrade from a .22 to a .38.

My man was living with me, even though some nights he didn't make it home. I didn't fuss when he came home. I wasn't one of those hoes that be stressing their man out so he would find a reason to run to the next bitch.

I was going to be his peace from the storm in his life. Plus, he just blessed me with a baby blue BMW. What else can a bitch ask for? I had everything I ever dreamed of—and more. The year 2006 was definitely my year to get my shine on those hoes in Richmond.

I had also been looking for a store to rent. My homegirl Li'l Mo' wanted to roll with me. We were two bad bitches with scissors and marcels. I was going to name the shop Millennium Stylez.

Alijah called and said he was on his way home. I decided to cook him some soul food. See, I wasn't a great cook, but I put my soul into cooking him some fried chicken, candy yams, collard greens, and corn on the cob. I hope he liked it.

After I cooked, I straightened up. I was still trying to get used to living in a big house. I glanced around. Hmm . . . It was a big come up from that little matchbox that I used to call home for the last twenty-one years. Now when I looked around, all I saw was wall-to-wall carpet, plasma TVs, and designer furniture. These were all the benefits of playing second. It didn't matter what he did. He was taking care of me, and I was playing my part as his ride-or-die chick.

Six hours later, he walked through the door and headed straight for the shower. I was feeling some type of way because he lied to me that he was coming straight home. I warmed his food up and put it on the table, then went to my room. I flipped through the channels. There was nothing that grabbed my attention, so I settled for the news on CNN.

He walked in the room in just his boxers. Damn, he looked sexy. That's the shit I was talking about. No matter how mad I was at him, I couldn't stay like that for long.

"Ma, you know I love you, right?"

"Sure," I said, then looked at him to make sure I was hearing him right.

"That's all you gon' say after I just put my feelin' out there?" He looked at me puzzled.

"What you want me to say, Alijah?"

He took my hand and turned my face toward him. "I know you tight wit' a nigga right now, but I'm handlin' the situation. It's gonna get better real soon, ma, just bear wit' a nigga," he pleaded. He paused, then continued, "You e'erything a nigga need. I see us together for a long-ass time," he said sincerely.

"Alijah, I love you too, and I'm tryin'a understand yo' situation, but it's hard. My feelings are involved."

"I feel you and give you my word. I'm workin' on it," he said while rubbing his hand over his braids.

"Don't worry, boo. I'm not going anywhere, unless you want me to," I assured him.

"That's what's good, 'cause I need you on my team."

That brought tears to my eyes because that was all new to me. I was always lacking love from when I was a child. Now I had a nigga that loved me. That was fucking great.

We ended up making love all night. Our bodies were drained. We were going to need some vitamin pills if we continued to fuck at the rate we were going.

"No bullshit, Sierra! I'm dead serious . . . If I eva catch you fuckin' wit' these lame-ass niggas out here, it's not gon' be pretty."

"I'm all yours, daddy. You ain't got to worry about me," I said mischievously.

Even though I tried to downplay the seriousness of what he said, deep down, I knew he meant every word that came out his mouth. As I lay my head on his chest, I wondered what I had gotten myself into.

I heard the phone ring even in my sleep. Dammit, who the hell was calling me? I peeped at the clock; it was three o'clock in the fucking morning.

"Hello," I said, sounding annoyed. "I *said* hello."

"Hello, who is this?" a female voice whispered.

"Listen, *you* called *my* damn phone, so what *you* want?"

"Oh, you must be the bitch that's sleeping with my husband."

This bitch caught me off guard, but I recognized the voice. I got out of the bed and tiptoed into the hallway, careful not to wake Alijah up.

"Nah, bitch, get it right. We're sleeping together, and how the fuck you got my number anyways?" I asked in a fierce tone.

"Just so you know, you're just another one of the flings. Don't feel special. He'll get tired of your stank ass soon," she stuttered.

"Listen up, you stalkin'-ass bitch. Don't be mad 'cause yo' man done replaced yo' saddity ass. Take that shit up wit' yo' husband. Oops! I forgot. That's right, he's right here in *my* bed."

I hung the phone up in that ho's face. I was heated. She got some fucking nerve calling my phone. I just knew I'd have to whup that ass sooner or later.

I used the bathroom and got back in bed beside my boo. My nerves were bad. I couldn't fall asleep because my cell kept ringing. This time, I didn't give a rat's ass if I woke Alijah up. Hell! The bitch was *his* fucking problem.

"Hello," I screamed at the top of my lungs.

"Who tha fuck was that, yo?" Alijah said, disgruntled.

"Why don't you ask yo' wife, and how the fuck she got my number?"

"That was Shayna?"

"Yup, she been callin' nonstop for the last ten minutes."

"Word?"

He got up, took his cell phone, and walked out of the room, closing the bedroom door behind him. I figured he wanted privacy. I ended up dozing off before he could finish with that psychotic bitch.

Alijah Jackson

Shayna went overboard when she called Sierra's phone. The bitch must've gone through my phone. I wondered what else she was digging into.

I really hated going off on her 'cause the drama that she went through, but she was gon' get it together or get the fuck outta my life. Every time we tried talking about it, it would turn into a fight with her putting her hands on me. I told her ass the next time I was gon' beat her ass down like Ike whupped Tina's ass.

By the time that I got up, Sierra was gone. I remembered her mentioning something 'bout getting her hair done. I took a shower, got dressed, and headed out to Chesterfield. I knew Shayna was still on her bullshit. It'd be nice when she returned to work. She had too much free time on her hands.

I parked my car in the driveway, just in case I needed to leave in a rush. As I walked through the house, it was like a tornado had just hit down. Things were all over the place. I walked in the living room where I figured she'd be since the TV was blasting. She was sitting on the couch humming some shit and rocking back and forth. The bitch was looking like the chick in *Fatal Attraction*, so I kept my distance.

"Yo, what you call me ova here fo'?" I asked wit' an attitude.

"You bastard! How could you treat me like this? I've stuck wit' yo' dirty black ass through everything, and *this* how you do me?"

"Yo, B, watch yo' mouth!" I warned.

"Or *what,* Alijah? You gon' beat my ass?"

"Nah, B, that'd be too easy. I'ma leave yo' crazy ass alone."

I must've hit a nerve 'cause this deranged bitch came full force off the sofa and tried to slap me in the face. I grabbed her arm.

"Shayna, keep yo' fuckin' hands to yourself, 'cause I already told you the next time, I'ma beat the life outta you."

I let her arm go as I stared down on her. I didn't recognize the person that was standing in front of me. When I met her, she was confident, catered to my needs, but after the miscarriage, she turned into a psycho bitch.

She started to cry. I wasn't gon' let her get to me, though. I was at the point where I didn't give a fuck. I was gonna cut my losses and keep it moving. If I stayed around, I was gon' end up hurting her—and not mentally but physically.

I stormed out of the house thinking, *Why the fuck did I come over here?* It was not worth the aggravation. I hated this stupid bitch.

Shayna Jackson

I had just finished downing my last drop of vodka, and I was pissy drunk. I kept replaying Vivian Green's "Emotional Roller Coaster" on the CD player. That's how my life felt lately. My marriage was in disarray. I tried calling Markus, but he didn't answer the phone. I was feeling drunk and horny.

I totally forgot that I had found the bitch's number that Alijah was fucking in his phone. So I dialed the number.

"Hello."

I was going to hang up, but I had to find out what was going on between those two. I got straight to the point with her sneaky ass, but the bitch laughed in my face as if I was a joke to her. It was a disaster. That bastard was in bed with her. The bitch had the nerve to hang up in my face. This hood bitch must not know who she was fucking with, and she better be prepared because she was in the big league now.

I kept calling her back-to-back. They were not going to enjoy each other's company on my time. I was pretty sure he was laid-back listening to that bitch disrespect me. Then he had the nerve to call me. I wasn't trying to hear his lying, cheating ass, so I hung up on him and crawled up into my bed, thinking tomorrow will be a better day.

The next day, this asshole had the nerve to show his fucking face. To make matters worse, he ridiculed me and put his fucking hands on me. He treated me like one of his hoes in the streets, but being the strong, motivated bitch I was, I drank some more and contemplated my next move.

Chapter Nine

Alijah Jackson

I stayed at the Telly with Luscious. I hadn't been giving her no time. I'd been occupied with Sierra's lovin' and Shayna's eccentric behavior.

Sierra kept blowin' up my phone, so I turned it off. Now wasn't the time to explain myself. I would deal with the consequences later.

Mami didn't speak much English, so we didn't have much of a conversation. Her actions spoke louder than her words. Her favorite line was "Mucho dinero, Papi." I didn't mind peeling her off 'cause her service was top quality.

I woke up lookin' around. That's when I remembered where I was. Shorty was in the shower. I grabbed my boxers and covered my naked behind. Shit, I had somewhere I needed to be. I cut my phone on. Fuck! I was late. It was past ten o'clock.

"Good morning, Papi."

"Whaddup, Ma?"

She came out of the bathroom in just her lacy drawers set, revealing her enticing, naked body. She gave me a half smile. If I wasn't rushing, I'd beat that pussy up one more time, but, nah, business came before pleasure, and I was already running late.

"You are leaving already?" she questioned in a mischievous tone.

"Yea, ma, I got some business to handle."

She looked at me disappointed. "Could you drop me off at the club, so I could pick up my car?"

"Sure, let's go." I handed her a thousand dollars.

"Thank you, Papi."

"No problem, Ma."

I dropped her off and headed back to the city. I was pushing almost 100 mph when I heard the jakes' siren behind me, and I pulled over. A big, burly, donut-eating pig walked toward my car. Without hesitation, I let the window down. I took out my license and registration.

"Hello, sir, were you aware you were going 95 mph in a 35 mph zone?"

"No, sir," I said, trying to be polite.

"License and registration, please."

I handed them to him. He headed back to his car. By now, his boy had showed up. I felt nervous, even though I knew I was straight. Luckily, I wasn't riding dirty. He came back and handed me my shit along with a ticket.

"Be more careful, young man," he warned.

"Thank you, sir. I'll take heed."

I pulled off slowly until I was out of sight. I dialed Sierra's number. I knew she was tight with me. I didn't have much time to waste. I had to meet up with this cat. He wanna cop half a brick. It was a big come up from the ozes he usually copped, but I was happy to see a little dude handlin' his B.I.

"Hello," Sierra answered the phone.

"Whaddup, ma? Before you get mad, lemme explain. I was jive busy handlin' some things."

"Whatever, Alijah, you ain't got to explain shit to me. You alive; that's all I was worried about."

I felt terrible. She sure deserved better than what I was dishing out.

"Ma, listen up. Look in the closet. You'll see a black duffel bag. Put in yo' pocketbook and bring it down. I need you to ride wit' me."

She didn't question me. That's one of the things I liked about Sierra. She wasn't into all that drama and headaches bitches be bringing to a nigga.

I let her drive. I was tired from all that fucking. I looked in my side mirror and peeped a dark-colored Sedan following us, ever since we hit Church Hill. I didn't recognize the car. I thought my mind was playing tricks on me 'cause the car disappeared when I glanced back in the mirror. I really needed to get this paranoia under control.

Sierra pulled over behind a Geo truck. Nothing seemed out of pocket, and my burner was in place, extra clips in my pocket. The door to the building was ajar. As I stepped foot in the door, I knew the vibe wasn't right, but it was a minute too late to back out.

Pop! Pop! Pop!

I didn't have time to pull my nine from my waist.

Sierra Rogers

I tossed and turned. I looked at the clock on the nightstand. His ass still didn't make it home, and his phone was turned off. This had become a pattern—couple days here, then he'd go MIA.

I wasn't stunting him because I was the one laid up in this brand-new crib with a brand-new car. I was the one fucking him any way his heart desired, or should I say, his dick desired. I was his Bottom Bitch.

I didn't have to go to work; the hot water tank broke. Charley should be ashamed of how he handles the business. All that money he was making off of us, and he still wouldn't invest in fixing up the shop. I found me a shop. I have to meet the landlord. I was getting impatient. The atmosphere at work was getting hostile, and I was ready to bust one of them hating-ass bitches in the head. Mark my words.

I took a shower even though I didn't have any plans. I threw some sweatpants on with a baby tee, made me some hot wings, kicked back, and started to watch Jerry Springer. They had some faggots on their rumbling. I was in need of a good laugh anyways.

When my phone started to ring, I answered it. It was Alijah on the other end trying to explain himself to me. I stopped him before he could finish lying to me. Whatever he was saying wasn't nothing but some irrelevant bullshit. I was happy that he was safe and sound.

He asked me to grab a bag and ride with him.

"Where we off to?" I questioned since I was the one driving.

"We are headin' 'round Church Hill," he said bluntly.

I handed him the bag, then I adjusted my seat and took off. I was no fool, and I knew that drugs were inside. I cut through Shockoe Bottom and was in Church Hill in no time.

"Yo, go down Thirty-second Street."

"Thirty-second?" I asked with confusion on my face. I wondered who he knew around there.

The niggas that lived on Thirty-first, Thirty-second, and Thirty-third were all known for their heartlessness. Danger was imminent. I kept my feelings to myself, though, and I hoped nothing was about to jump off.

"Pull over right here and keep the engine runnin'. I'll be out in a minute."

I watched as he disappeared into the building. The number on the apartment said 600 N. Thirty-second Street. A dark blue Cadillac Seville drove by. I tried to see inside, but the windows were tinted black.

A feeling of uneasiness rushed over me. I opened my pocketbook; my .22 was intact. It wasn't no match for the big burners, but that wasn't going to stop me from trying. I kept looking toward the door. I saw no sign of Alijah. All I heard were back-to-back gunshots ring out from inside the apartment that Alijah went into. I saw two niggas with ski masks haul ass; then I heard tires screeching. It was the same car from earlier. The two dudes jumped in the car and sped off. I caught the license plate before they turned the corner onto Leigh Street.

There was still no sign of Alijah. Fuck that. I jumped out and ran into the apartment that was wide open. With my weapon in my hand, I ran toward where the sound came from. I didn't know what lay ahead for me. All I knew was that my man was up in there possibly hurt or even dead.

"Aagh, aagh," I heard someone groan.

"Alijah! Alijah!"

Still no answer.

Damn, it was stinking in there. This was nothing but a smitty. Damn, I knew then it was set up. They set Alijah up.

"Ma, I'm right here in the back," a faint voice echoed.

"Alijah! Alijah!" I rushed to the back of the house. "Oh my God. Oh my God!"

Alijah was lying there with blood all over him.

"What happened, baby?"

He looked at me. "Them niggas robbed me, ma. I'm shot."

"Where they shoot you at?"

"I think my stomach," he said, with his voice fading away.

"Stay with me, Alijah," I begged while tears flowed down my face.

"Come on, boo, let's get you to the car."

Now, this boy was built, so I didn't know where the strength came from. I put one of his arms over my shoulder to hold his weight up. He fought to keep up with me. I practically dragged him into the Jeep. He kept moaning.

"Ma, did you get the burner?"

"Yup, it's right here." I had it in my coat pocket.

I reversed back, then pulled off. I thought about calling the ambulance but decided not to. I was taking him to the hospital. As I looked back at him lying on the backseat, I noticed him falling in and out of consciousness.

"God, no, please don't do this," I whispered a prayer to God.

I took his gun out of my coat and put it in my pocketbook. I was sure going to jail if they searched me, but this wasn't the time to be selfish. My man's life was on the line. I ran every red light on my way to MCV. I pulled into the emergency entrance, jumped out, and started to yell.

"Help! Help! My boyfriend is shot."

They must've heard me because they came running from all angles.

"What happened, ma'am?" a policeman asked me.

I showed him Alijah. "He's shot in the stomach."

"Please, get back," a doctor said, rushing over.

They put him on a stretcher and started to check his pulse.

"He's breathing; we got a pulse," a nurse confirmed.

They rushed him to the back of the emergency room. Then the police officer came to me. "Ma'am, please come with us."

I followed them outside.

"So, tell us what happened to your friend."

It wasn't my place to tell them what happened. See, Alijah didn't have much love for the po-po, so I was going to wait. I really hoped he pulled through. Then if he wanted to, he could talk to them, even though I doubted that.

After the detectives saw that they weren't getting anywhere with me, they gave me their card, in case I had a change of heart. God was on my side because the bastards didn't search me.

I went outside to get some air. That's when I broke down. I wasn't the holiest person in the world, but I got down on my knees and started to pray to the Almighty. I couldn't lose Alijah; we just got started. I wanted to get married and have a whole bunch of badass kids.

I felt a hand on my shoulder. I quickly turned around, ready to knock the fuck out of whoever it was. I put my fist down, though, when I saw it was an older lady with silver hair smiling down at me. My first thought was *Who is this old bitch invading my space?*

"Listen, lady, this isn't a good time," I said, using my hands to wipe away the mucus that was running down my nose.

"Chile, the Lord doesn't give you more than you can bear. Give him whatever you dealing wit'. He'll take care of it." She placed her arm on my shoulder. "Pray about it, and it will be all right," she said in the most sincere tone.

It might've been a mind thing, but I felt like a burden was suddenly lifted off of me. I turned around to thank her, but she was gone. I looked around, but it was as if she was never there.

It was exactly one o'clock in the morning, and I was still in the waiting room trying to get an update on Alijah. Earlier, I went through his phone and called his boy, Darryl. Even though I never met him, I knew Alijah would want him there. He came with three other dudes. They couldn't see him because he was still in surgery. Darryl was heated. He just paced back and forth. I tried explaining the little I knew. All the while, he kept swearing he was going to kill whoever was responsible for touching his brother. I saw the venom in his eyes when he spoke.

His boy, Chuck, had the audacity to question *me* about where *I* was when his boy was getting shot up. See, I knew what he was trying to imply.

"Nigga, I was where he told me to be," I said with a serious look on my face.

The time that they were wasting by being up in my face, they should have been out getting at the niggas who were responsible for hurting their boss.

"Miss, your friend is finally out of surgery. He's in the ICU. Follow me."

Alijah was lying in the bed. If it wasn't for his name tag, I wouldn't have recognized him. He was swollen, with all those tubes running through his body, and his color was a dark purple. Tears rolled down my cheeks. I touched him on his face. He was asleep, so I just stood there looking at him.

"Miss, your friend here is a fighter. He took three bullets to the abdomen. We lost him twice, but between his will to live and our experience, he's still with us. However, with gunshot victims, the first seventy-two hours are critical, but I have faith he'll be all right."

"Thank you, Doctor." I shook his hand. I could really kiss him for saving my man's life.

I stayed with him until about seven the next morning. I kept talking to him, even though it was a one-sided conversation. When I decided to leave, I kissed him on the forehead and left. I wanted to stay by his side, but the doctor said I wouldn't be much help to him, so I decided to go home and get myself together. But, believe I was going to be the first one there when he opened his eyes.

The police took his car for pending investigation, so I called me a cab. As I stepped out in the early-morning breeze, loneliness and sadness came upon me. *This is not happening,* I thought as I jumped in the cab.

Shayna Jackson

I was on the treadmill trying to get my body toned. Not that I needed it, but I had to keep myself up. My phone started to ring a few times. I ignored it, but it kept constantly ringing.

It was Markus on the other end telling me that Alijah had got shot the day before. His friends were so disrespectful that I was the last to hear about it. I should've been the first. He also rubbed in my face that Alijah was with that slut when he met his bullets. It served his cheating ass just right. They should've put a slug in her ass too. I might seem cruel, but the bitch was in the way of me getting all the money.

I called Ms. Sharon, Alijah's mom. She broke down crying. I tried to console her the best way I knew. She had a lot of questions, but I was like her—in the dark. She was on the next plane to Richmond.

I got to the hospital in no time.

"Hello, I'm here to see my husband, Alijah Jackson. He was admitted yesterday."

"Sure, ma' am, let me see some identification."

I took my license out and handed it to the clerk.

Alijah was asleep when I got there. Somehow, I felt a little pity for him. I was surprised the cops weren't all over his room. The doctor came and gave me an update. I stayed for about half an hour; then I left. I really didn't want to be there. I just had to go see for myself.

I knew that when a person was shot, security was tight at the hospital, so I went ahead and put Sierra Rogers down as his keep away. *I* was the wife, so *I* would be there. I'd love to see the look on her face when she realized that she couldn't visit him.

After I left the hospital, I phoned Markus. We needed to get together and discuss numbers. I wanted to know what Alijah's personal account looked like. I was his wife, so if he kicked the bucket, I'd be the sole beneficiary. Sounds good to me. I'd finally be a filthy rich widow, enjoying my fortune somewhere on an exotic island with a young foreign stallion.

Markus showed up with Alijah's financial statements. In our joint account, we had more than 2.5 million, but to my surprise, he had a dummy account with over 5 million, plus stocks and bonds. My heart skipped a beat. I never figured in a lifetime that we were *that* rich.

While we were going over the paperwork, I saw that Markus wasn't looking too pleased.

"What's the matter?"

"I've been waiting patiently on you, but it seems like you have no plans to leave Alijah."

I walked around his side of the desk and put my arm around his shoulder. "I do want to be with you, but I just found out my husband been holding out on me. I'm not going anywhere until I get all that's rightfully mine."

"I just want us to leave. I feel guilty doing this to my boy. You promised it'd only be a couple of times. Well, this been damn well over a couple. I'm telling you, Shayna, Alijah ain't no fool. He's going to find out sooner than later."

"Listen up, you little wimp, *I'm* calling the shots. *I* decide when it's enough. Until then, keep your comments to yourself."

"You're one coldhearted bitch. How did I ever allow myself to get caught up in your web of deceit? Stay the fuck away from me," he warned. He stormed out of the house and got in his Camry.

"A coldhearted bitch? Ha! You haven't seen *anything* yet." I closed my door, thinking of a master plan.

Chapter Ten

Alijah Jackson

I woke up, looked around, and didn't recognize my surroundings. I tried to get up, but my body was sore to the point where I couldn't move without feeling excruciating pain. Then I remembered I got shot, and Sierra was driving me to the hospital. Everything else was a blur.

A nurse walked in the room. "Good morning, Mr. Jackson. How are you feeling this morning?"

I wanted to blurt out, "Bitch, how you *think* I'm feeling?" but decided against it. Instead, I said, "You tell me, Nurse Webb."

"Well, the doctor will be here later this morning to discuss your prognosis with you. In the meantime, I'll be taking your vitals, and the nurse's aide will be in to help with your bath."

After she left the room, I slipped into deep thought. I swore on everything I loved, I was going to hunt them little niggas down and body them. I had to give it to them; they had a lot of guts, but they made a major mistake.

Minutes later, the nurse returned followed by two dudes dressed in suits. I knew off top they were DTs. You could put clothes on a pig, but underneath, he was still a swine. I put my game face on, ready to be attacked, probably arrested. I hadn't heard from Sierra, so I wasn't sure if they found my burner or the extra clip.

"Mr. Jackson, that's your name, right?"

"You already know what it is, so what's good?"

"For a person who just escaped death, you sure have a nasty demeanor."

"Exactly my point. I just got shot, so why you up in here harassing me? Shouldn't you be out there findin' whoever did this to me?" I asked harshly.

I knew that statement would give them something to think about, at least for the time being. I wondered where the fuck Sierra was at. We needed to be on the same page about that shit.

"Hold! Hold! We just trying to do our job. Don't bust our bubbles here," the other piglet jumped in.

"Bottom line is I got shot, and I have no idea who did it."

"Mr. Jackson, if your life is in danger, we can protect you."

"Nah, my life is not in danger, but I'm feelin' weak. I'd like for y'all to leave so I can get some rest, gentlemen." I pointed toward the door.

"Well, here's my card. If you remember anything that can help us get the person that did this to you, please feel free to contact me."

Minutes later, my crew walked in. I was so happy to see some familiar faces. They all gave me daps.

"First thing first, bruh, how you feelin'?"

"I'm livin', so I'm good. I'm waitin' to get up wit' tha doc," I said, trying to sound hard.

"Yo, bruh, what tha fuck happen, and who did it?" Dre questioned.

"Son, it's crazy. Li'l dude, C-Lo, that I been fuckin' wit', called me, said he needed half a brick. My first instinct say don't fuck wit' him 'cause he don't have that type of paper. But for real, he reminded me of myself when I first started out, so I decided to meet him."

"Yo, what the bitch had to do wit' it?" Dre questioned with anger.

"Who you talkin' 'bout? Sierra? Nah, she rode wit' me over there."

"Yo, son! Everybody suspect right 'bout now, you heard," Chuck joined in.

"Son, I feel you, but shorty don't get down like that. She's the only reason that I'm breathin' right now."

I saw where the conversation was heading. My niggas only meant well. I couldn't let Sierra get caught up in what was about to jump off, even though I was surprised she wasn't up there visiting me. Deep down, I knew she was my ride-or-die chick.

"Yo, son, the second I entered the building, shit seemed off. For one, dude said that was his crib, but that shit was a smitty. Now that I think 'bout it, dude had no intention to cop. It was all a setup. I didn't get a chance to hit back; it happened so fast."

"Yo, Boss, we gon' handle them niggas."

"Nah, y'all need to chill out till I get outta this bitch. This is personal, so I'ma handle it."

"A'ight, Boss, it's your call, but we ready," Dre warned.

I knew he was ready; him and Chuck were stone-cold killers. I knew they were ready to turn Richmond upside down, but I couldn't have that. It would be bad for business. We had to be careful. If not, we all were gonna be dead or locked up; neither one of those was an option for me.

In the midst of our conversation, Shayna walked in. The look on my niggas' faces revealed they were ready to exit the building.

"Hello, everyone," she said, rollin' her eyes.

They paid her no mind as usual. It's been bad blood between her and the crew, but out of the respect for me, the guys didn't carry her like a regular no-good bitch.

"Yo, we out. We be back tomorrow. Get some rest. Stay sucker free," Darryl said while eyeing Shayna.

They all left. I knew Shayna was hot by her evil looks.

"Hey, baby." She came over and gave me a kiss on the cheek.

I didn't respond.

"I hope you're feeling much better. Your mom is on her way as we speak."

"You called her?"

"Yes, I believe she needs to know what's going on with her only child."

I just shook my head.

"Baby, I can't wait until you feel better. I almost lost you, so I have decided to be a better woman so you won't cheat anymore." She started to cry. "Did you like all the flowers I had delivered?"

"Sure, thank you." Until she said something 'bout the flowers, I hadn't really noticed. Now when I looked at them, they reminded me of a funeral home. That bitch was already planning my funeral. I was hoping her ass didn't show up.

She stayed for a couple of more hours, popping nothing but bullshit. I was out by the time she left. She paid for my phone before she left. I called Sierra, but it went straight to voice mail. I needed to talk to her ASAP. The pain was kicking my ass, so I kept pushing the morphine button. The nurse also gave me some Percocet. I was high as a kite, and some good herb would've made it better. I dozed off without hearing from my girl.

Sierra Rogers

Ever since Alijah had gotten shot, I'd been at the hospital, but he still was in a coma. I would just sit in the chair and talk to him. The doctor said although he was unresponsive, he might still be able to hear me talking to him.

I tried to be strong for him while I was there, but at night, when I was all alone, I broke down. I couldn't even remember the last time I had a meal, and I took time off from work so I could go back and forth to the hospital.

I was up bright and early. Darryl called and told me that Alijah was up and asking for me. I gave my ID to the attendant like I usually did. Shockingly, he told me I couldn't visit him because my name was on the no-visit list.

"Yo, you makin' a mistake. Could you please check again! The name is S-i-e-r-r-a R-o-g-e-r-s." I even spelled it out for him. He seemed irritated, but I didn't give a damn. I was trying to go see my boo.

"Well, Ms. Rogers, we were asked not to let you anywhere near the patient. You're considered dangerous to his recovery. If you continue to be persistent, I have no choice but to call security and have you put off the premises."

It was useless to continue arguing with that clown. I was annoyed as hell. Why would I be considered dangerous to Alijah? I knew I didn't have anything to do with what had happened to him. My heart was aching. I just needed to see him, to let him know I had nothing to do with him getting shot.

I got in my car and started to drive. I didn't want to go home, so I drove to the James River. I got out and started to walk. It was so peaceful down there. I passed a couple who were holding hands; they seemed so in love. It seemed like any hope I had of Alijah's and my happiness was quickly fading. Our life had been nothing less than turmoil since we got together.

The nights without my man were harder than I had imagined. I started to have nightmares, jumping out of my sleep, crying at times. I'd be scared to go back to sleep. I knew I had done a lot of grimy shit in my life, but I didn't deserve what life was throwing at me.

I was at the gas station filling my car up. Damn, gas was on the rise in Richmond, and so was crime. The mayor was on the television earlier talking about we needed to pull together and fight crime. Shit, the government was the ones that gave the guns to the youths in the community. I'd see mothers burying their sons every day.

It really hit home when Alijah got shot. It made me realize what a dangerous world we lived in. In my heart, I wanted to change the way I was living, but that's the only way I'd known. You can call me a product of my environment. I couldn't turn back. I'd always been a rider, so it was no different, and I was going to ride until the wheels fell off.

Later that evening, I answered the phone. It was Alijah. He was as shocked about the block on the visiting list as I was. We both concluded that Shayna's bitch ass did it. I was happy just to hear his voice. An hour later, he called and told me he handled the problem. I was on the way.

I stepped up to the desk. This time around the attendant was much friendlier.

"I'm sorry 'bout the other day. It was a big misunderstanding."

I bet it was. Alijah probably screamed at their boss, who, in turn, screamed at their asses.

"No problem. I'm just happy it's cleared up."

I headed to the elevator. I was excited to see my man, just to hold him for a quick second. I stepped out of the elevator and headed to room 307. Quickly, I looked down to make sure my clothes were straight, and when I looked back up, there was a woman standing in the doorway. I figured that she was one of the staff at the hospital. In any case, she needed to move her ass out of the way.

"Excuse me, um . . . I need to get in the room."

"No. Excuse *you*. This is *my* son's room, and *no one* is allowed to visit unless they family or the staff here," she said with an attitude.

That's when it hit me that this was his mom. She looked innocent like an angel, but her stare was colder than an iceberg.

"Well, ma'am, I'm Sierra, Alijah's friend. He asked me to come up here."

"Mmm . . . You're the home wrecker that's trying to break up my son's marriage. You have a nerve showing your face up in here."

I was shocked. I wondered who the fuck the bitch was talking to in that manner.

"You know, lady! I don't *know* you, and you *definitely* don't know who *I* am. So, let's just go on 'bout our business and pretend this little conversation never took place," I said and mean mugged the old lady. She was lucky she was his mom 'cause I didn't discriminate. If the bitch was old enough to run her mouth, she was old enough to get her ass whupped.

"Listen, you little tramp. I could smell your cheapness from a mile away. Stay out of my son's life. Shayna is a virtuous woman and deserves a chance to work out her marriage."

"Ms. Jackson, or whatever your name is, as far as I'm concerned, lady, I don't care about her or their marriage. I love Alijah, and he loves me, and for the record, I'm not leaving him any time soon."

I must've gotten my point across because she stepped out of the doorway. I walked in with a fake smile on my face. I didn't want to add more stress to Alijah. I sat on the bed beside him. He looked much better than when I last saw him. He was one lucky nigga. God was definitely on his side.

He told me his mom had just left. I didn't even respond. I kept looking toward the door expecting her or Shayna to bust up in there at any second. I was prepared for a showdown. They needed to know they were wasting their time, and I was not backing down.

Alijah Jackson

It had been five weeks, and I was finally out of the hospital. Mom-dukes hadn't left my side. This made it harder for Sierra to come visit.

Shayna must've put a bug in her ear 'cause she tried to talk to me about how I was treating Shayna. I shut her down 'fore she got too far. *I* was the one that had to deal with that crazy-ass bitch, but like always, Shayna had her fooled, just like she did everyone else.

My recovery was comin' along well. I had a nurse coming out to the house. I was staying in the guest room. Even though Shayna was pretending like the caring wife, I knew better. I lost my strength, not my memory. In front of people, she pretended to be the doting partner. I didn't want to let my mom down, so for the time being, I played along with her gimmicks.

I stayed on the phone most of the time with Sierra. I knew she felt some type of way that I wasn't home, but I assured her things would get better soon, then we'd be together.

It became overbearing with my mom around all the time. I had to let her know I was not crippled. She got the picture and decided to head back to New York.

Darryl kept things under control. He made the necessary trips up top. Saleem and the fellas dropped by daily to show their love. Saleem kept me updated on what was going on in the streets. He also told me the niggas were bragging 'bout how they reached out and "touched the big man." That made me determined to get my strength back. I was ready for a showdown. I had enough guns and ammo to wipe out that little-ass town.

Saleem also put up fifty grand on each of their heads. They had to know that their life was coming to an end, especially when money was involved.

Shayna wasn't too pleased when the fellas came over. We'd kick back and chill. They would smoke blunt after blunt. I was ordered not to smoke. Even though we never discussed the shooting since I been home, I knew it was still fresh on each of our minds.

***

The kid was back like cooked crack with the help of my sexy, young therapist. Shorty had a body on her that made a nigga dick rock hard by just lookin'. If Shayna wasn't in the way, I'd get at her fo' sure.

I was back to my living arrangement between the new houses. I couldn't wait to get up in some pussy. I was feeling horny like a pit bull when Shayna walked in the room. She looked like she was putting on some weight 'cause she was thicker than a Snicker. I couldn't resist the temptation. I pulled her down on the bed with me and started to kiss on her. We ended up fucking, and boy did she perform. I was shocked. It was the new and improved Shayna.

We ended up fucking nonstop for a good two hours. She tried her best to leave marks and scratches on me. I already peeped what she was doing; trying to let it be known that we was fucking.

Later that night, I went home to Sierra. She cooked me dinner, but the only thing that I wanted to eat was what she had between her legs. I got a crazy feeling whenever I was around her. But first, I got in the shower. I couldn't risk her smelling Shayna's perfume all over me.

She must've read my mind because when I entered the bedroom, she was sprawled out on her back butt naked with her legs wide open, playing with her pussy. The scene alone had me drunk mentally. I dove onto the bed, putting my face between her goods. The smell alone drove me crazy. I had to taste her garden of sweetness.

I seductively sucked on her clit, then went in deeper for the kill with my razor tongue. It was her night to get satisfied to the highest level of lovemaking. I watched as she had multiple orgasms. As her body shivered uncontrollably, she pleaded with me for the dick. I totally ignored her cries. I had her where I wanted her; then I slid my wood in slowly. It was wetter and tighter than the last time I'd hit it. The look on her face let me know I was hurting her, so I eased up a little. If it was another broad, I wouldn't give a fuck, but that was my future wife. I couldn't treat her like that. We fucked all night, just like old times.

I made two trips up top since I had been back on my grind. A few days ago, I had a safe built in the basement at Sierra's house. I started to stash some paper down there. Just in case anything happened to me, she'd be taken care of.

Something else was bothering me too. It was kind of strange. After the shooting, all the guys rallied around me except Markus. I saw him once when we had a meeting. I wondered what was really good with holmes.

I went directly to his crib. He stayed over on the South Side. Whatever was bothering him must be serious because of his eccentric behavior. I knocked a couple of times before he opened the door. He had an odd look on his face.

"Oh, what's up, Boss? What a surprise." He gave me a half-broken smile. I also noticed his demeanor was weird.

"Yo, B, can I come in?" I didn't wait for a response. I walked by him, inviting myself into his crib. "What you been up to, son?"

"Nuttin', just takin' care a business like you pay me to," he replied with a devilish grin.

Somehow I felt sump'n wasn't right with duke. We had been around each other long enough to know when shit ain't right.

"Word? Well, if you say e'erything cool, then that's what is then. Yo, you keepin' my paper straight?"

"Everything legit; all the money there," he assured me.

I peeped how he kept twitching in his chair. He was showing signs of nervousness. If I wasn't mistaken, he had beads of sweat on his forehead.

I made a mental note to go through my finances with a magnifying glass ASAP. I had a gut feelin' that our business and personal relations were about to be terminated—on bad terms.

"Yo, check this out, son. You throwin' off a bad vibe. I 'on't know what it is, but I intend to get to the bottom of whatever it is that's having you bugged out like this." I got up to leave before I hurt dude without having solid proof. "Yo, son, I'm out. Lemme know what's good." I walked out without a response.

I could've been wrong 'bout duke, but me knowing him for the last eight years, his two major worries were getting money and getting pussy. I knew for a fact his money was straight 'cause we were eating good, and as for bitches, he ain't no playa, but he gets by. The fellas usually clowned that he was an undercover batty man, but that was yet to be proven.

I finally hooked up with Luscious. She had been blowing my phone up since I got out of the hospital. I knew she wanted to get fucked, but I gave her the runaround. Sierra kept a nigga in the house with her good cooking and her off-the-wall lovemaking.

I lied to Sierra about my whereabouts. I didn't have to worry 'bout Shayna 'cause they said, "All good things shall come to an end." After fucking Shayna, she transformed like that chick in *The Exorcist,* but that didn't stop me from doing me.

It was like every time that I got with shorty, I ended up staying the night. She must have been working some type of Puerto Rican voodoo that pulled me closer to her. She made sure it was all about me when we were together. Nothing else mattered.

It was a special night. She brought along one of her slut friends. I was kind of suspicious at first. Two hoes together couldn't be nothing but trouble. I really hoped their intention wasn't bad 'cause I didn't discriminate. I had no problem with clapping both their asses.

I was being careful 'cause we were in Sierra's neck of the woods. I got us enough liquor and smoke. I had a feeling that I was in for a treat with those two bad bitches.

I got right by smoking some Haze, but I didn't drink. You can call me paranoid, but it was two of them and one of me. Plus, they kept talkin' in their language.

After they got fucked up with the smoke and liquor, they wasted no time on eating each other's coochie in a 69 position. It was just like live porn, and they were some certified freaks. I kind of felt jealous when they left me out of the scene. That didn't last long, though, because they then turned their attention to me.

"Don't be scared, Papi," shorty, whose name was Candi, said as she licked her full set of lips. If she was anything like her name, I was in for a treat.

Just when I thought I'd experienced everything about sex 101, I was surprised at having two broads lick me down at the same time. They licked from head to toe, ass to balls, and took turns sucking on my dick as if they were famished. Luscious even stuck her tongue in my shit hole. I jumped, but when I felt her moist tongue, I felt like screaming out like I was a bitch. It didn't take long for me to bust off. It was a fucking sight to watch both them bitches compete to catch the flow of my unborn seeds.

The show wasn't over yet. I was eager to get between Candi's legs, and when I did get the chance, it wasn't like I anticipated. Bottom line, shorty had some garbage. Her shit was loose as hell. I kept edging it, but couldn't find the walls. It was a waste of my energy, so I pulled out. I turned on Luscious. I flipped her onto her stomach and started long dicking her. I was tight 'bout her friend's loose pussy, so I took it out on Luscious by beating that pussy up.

After all the excitement died down, we were drained. I was good, though. That bitch left after I threw her two bills. She gave me a look like *what is this?* I stared back almost ready to snatch my paper out of her hands. She got the pic and pranced out the door.

"You know yo' girl pussy was some straight garbage. For real. Her head game was the only reason I gave her that paper."

She didn't respond. We ended up smoking some more and fucked again. Pussy can sure knock a nigga out 'cause I didn't rise 'til one o'clock the next day. We went at it again, and then got dressed.

Darryl called in the process. I allowed Luscious to ride with me since her car was parked at Bigga Detailing Shop. When we walked in, shorty was seated on his lap.

"My bad, am I interruptin' sump'n?" I asked jokingly.

"Nah, bruh, my baby was just leavin'. Ladies, feel free to get acquainted," Darryl said.

I gave him dap, and we sat down at the bar. He sipped on a Heineken. I ordered me a flavored water. I had been trying to stay away from all the drinking since I got out of the hospital.

"Whaddup with baby girl?" I inquired.

"Same shit, different bitch. You know, smash, then quit," he bragged.

She must've heard him because she rolled her eyes at him. Darryl had a way with the chicks. It was nauseating. He called them all kind of hoes and tricks. You would think they'd leave him alone. Instead, they did the opposite—flock around him like fly on shit.

I couldn't compete with his smoothness with the ladies.

"Yo, son, you look like you been out all night."

"You know it. We been at the Telly."

"Word? I see you still fuckin' wit' her phat ass. You sure know how to keep a ho around."

"Yup, she the best piece a pussy fo' sale."

"Ha-ha, I hear you talkin', bruh. Better you than me 'cause you definitely got yo' hands full."

"I got it, bruh. It take a nigga like me to have shit unda control. I'ma leave Shayna's ass alone fo' good, though. I tell you, she one naggin'-ass bitch."

"I know that's right, playa. I told you from day one that bitch was a certified nutcase."

We both busted out laughing.

"Enough 'bout these hoes. Let's rap 'bout some serious shit. I did a house call on Markus yesterday."

"Holmes a'ight?"

"That's what I'm tryin'a find out."

"Now that you mention it, he been actin' kinda weird lately. It started right after you got hit."

"Word?" I said, shaking my head.

"Yo, you 'on't think holmes have anything to do wit' the hit?"

"Nah, ain't no way possible for him to know these little niggas, but, yo, check around and see if there's a link."

"You already know if anything comes up on duke, he going back home in a body bag."

"Yea, his moms better start makin' plans to bury the newest arrival—her muthafuckin' son."

Now that that was out of the way, we kicked it for a little while longer; then we bounced. I drove to where ole girl car was parked. She got out, and I handed her two grand.

"Thank you, Papi," she said and gave me a hug.

It would be one move that I ended up regretting.

Sierra Rogers

It had been a rocky road since Alijah got shot. He finally made it home, but his crazy-ass mama kept cock blocking. I guess trying to be funny.

I wasn't feeling all the drama that surrounded our lives. At times, I wondered if it would ever get better; would I be able to live a normal life with him? Whenever I related my concern to him, he would just assure me everything was going to get better. It was hard for me to digest any of it.

I finally met the landlord for my new spot. The space was much bigger than Charley's place. The price was a bit steep, but with me and Li'l Mo's clientele, we should be able to handle the bills. Charley wasn't happy when I told him I was leaving, but, hey, a bitch had to move on to bigger and better things. Eventually, he gave me his blessing.

A lot of people were talking about Alijah's situation. See, a lot of them didn't know we fucked with each other, so when the shit happened, bitches were gossiping as if they knew him. One bitch made a remark that she heard from her cousin, "He had a big dick." I wanted to two-piece that ho. I wondered who the fuck her cousin was. So, when they left, Jasmine old hypocrite self walked over to me.

"Gurl, I hope you not payin' that no mind."

This bitch was faker than a three-dollar bill. She knew damn well she didn't like me; more like jealous of me since high school.

"Nah, boo, I'm not studying that bitch, but I sure would like to know who her cousin is."

I threw it out there knowing that Jasmine's grimy ass couldn't hold water.

"Gurl, her cousin name Luscious. She's a stripper at Paper Moon."

"Oh really? That bitch just stuttin' like she fuckin' a real player like Alijah."

In my heart, I was thinking something else. I wondered when Alijah met her. I knew he frequented the strip joint, but for real, I didn't put nothing past a nigga. I sure hoped there wasn't no truth to the story, but it sure had me feeling some type of way.

Finally, everything in my life was getting back to normal. My man was back, and it was just like old times again. We started back on our regular fuck sessions. I was really in need of some good lovemaking, and, boy, he laid it down.

I was finally in my own spot too. The banner said Si' and Mo' Millennium Stylez. I had flyers made. I had to reach out to the young and old. I wasn't discriminating. A good hairstylist could turn an ugly duckling into a beauty queen.

I held a shop-warming party. Most of my clients came through, along with Mo's peoples.

Charley came through to show some love and talked shit at the same time. It was a'ight 'cause we talked shit right back at him. We had everything from barbeque chicken, fried fish, and barbeque ribs. It was a good feeling to see all those people showing us love.

It was surprising not to see Neisha. I tried to call her, but she didn't answer, so I went ahead and left her a message. The fact that I hadn't heard from her in a minute weighed heavily on me. I sensed some type of jealousy on her part ever since I told her about Alijah. It wasn't my fault she didn't find her a nigga with major paper.

I tried to school her on how to tighten up her game, but she wasn't trying to learn. There was an old saying, "You can lead a cow to the pond, but can't force him to drink." Fuck that! I was all for self now. My happiness came first. I've lived the worst of life. Now, I was living the best that life had to offer. If the bitch couldn't be happy for me, then she could continue staying the fuck away from me.

Lately, Alijah was buried deep in his thoughts. He had a lot on his mind, and I also knew that he was plotting on how to get back at the niggas that shot him. Every time that I thought about the inevitable, my heart ached. I knew nothing good was going to come out of it, and I didn't want to lose my baby. I agreed that he had to avenge the shooting. I just wished they'd hurry up and handle the situation because I was scared every time he stepped foot out the door.

It was a slow day. I didn't have much to do but a wash and set and two full weaves. Mo' left earlier to go hook up with some nigga she met a few days ago. We had been chilling more outside of work. She was mad funny. She clowned on niggas every chance she got. We had a lot in common. We both loved money and weren't going to fuck no broke-ass nigga. Li'l Boosie was talking about us when he rapped about I-N-D-E-P-E-N-D-E-N-T females.

I was trying to get downtown before the rush-hour traffic started. *Richmond sure got a lot of traffic*, I thought. Hull Street was jammed up too, so I cut through South Side Plaza and headed down Midlothian Turnpike. I made a left when I got to the intersection of Hull/Midlothian Turnpike.

I dialed Alijah's number. He didn't come home the night before and didn't call. That was the part of the deal that came with a hustler; they stayed gone most of the time.

The light was on red, so I stopped. That's when I peeped Alijah's Range Rover. That bright-ass color I could spot from a distance. It was parked outside of a car detailing shop. When the light changed, I decided to drive slow to see if he was outside, but the bitch behind me kept honking her horn, so I turned in the parking lot.

I spotted Alijah standing on the side of his ride, and a light-skinned, thick bitch was hugging on him. I didn't even bother to park! I jumped out and stormed toward them.

"Who tha fuck is this bitch all over you?" I pointed my finger in his face, but before he could respond, this two-dollar ho put her two cents in.

"Bitch, I'm Luscious," she spat.

See? I always believe in fight now, then ask questions later. I jumped on that ho like I was Bruce Lee. I two-pieced her ass, knocking her to the ground, then started stomping her with my fresh pair of Tims. The bitch tried to get back on her feet, but she wasn't no comparison to my rage.

I continued stomping that bitch while she screamed for Alijah. He didn't pay her any mind. All the frustration that was built up in me for the last twenty years, I took out on that ho. I had a flashback from the time that my mama left me hungry to the times that niggas played me. I gave that bitch the business.

Finally, Alijah tried to grab me away from that bitch, whose face was now bloody from my Tims. I turned around in rage and pushed him in the chest. “Keep yo’ fuckin’ hands off me, you hear me!” I was spitting fire.

I looked around for my Coach bag. As soon as I saw it, I snatched it up and pulled out my brand-new .38 I just copped at the gun show on Sunday and pointed it straight at his head.

“So, this your new bitch? Ha! You fuckin’ playin’ me with this ho. This how you doing yours?”

“Yo, ma, unless you intend to use it, get that shit out of my fuckin’ face,” he warned while walking toward me.

“Nah, fuck you, nigga! You ain’t worth it. This the last fuckin’ time you playin’ me for a fool. I’m good now; clean yo’ bitch up,” I said and walked away once again. I could hear him calling me, but I kept it moving.

I got in my car and sped off. This time I didn’t cry. Actually, it kind of felt good whooping that ho’s ass. Bitches didn’t know I was a beast with my hands, and I knew how to bust a gun if it came down to it.

As I drove home, Alijah kept blowing up my phone. I decided to turn it off 'cause I didn't want to hear shit that came out of his mouth. I got home and took my clothes off. That's when I realized that the bitch somehow managed to scratch my face and some parts on my neck. I put some peroxide on 'cause God knows what that bitch might have with her stanking ass.

I hoped his ass was smart enough to have worn rubbers. I would kill him if I ever caught anything. I was going tell his ass to go get tested. Shit, HIV was on the rise in Richmond, especially in the ghetto, and I be damned if I was going to become victim.

I called Mo', and we talked about the shit. She was angry that she wasn't there when it popped off. I had to convince her that her girl put it down on that ho. That bitch looked a hot mess when I left. She should be up in the hospital by now. Good for her ass. I was checking my nigga, and her bold ass wanted to jump in. She done lost her fucking mind.

Me and Mo' clowned for another fifteen minutes, then hung up. I was happy to have her in my life. I don't know what I would've done without her.

I was beat. I wasn't used to throwing blows no more. From that point on, if a bitch wanted to get at me, they could holler at Mr. .38 first.

I put Keyshia Cole's CD in and pressed repeat on "Love." Then I fell in a trance thinking about my life, the past, the present, and the future.

Chapter Eleven

Alijah Jackson

Man, fuck! I needed to tighten up on my game. I didn't expect Sierra to roll up on me like she did. I really didn't give a fuck 'bout the beat down that she put on ole girl. The bitch should've kept her mouth shut and minded her own fuckin' business.

Sierra took it a little bit too far when she disrespected me and pulled the burner on me. See, I don't know what kind of punk-ass nigga she was used to, but in my world, it was a violation. I'ma have to check her ass 'bout that shit.

Sierra wasn't tryin'a hear when I told her I wasn't cheating on her. See, unknown to me, Luscious's dumb-ass cousin was up in the shop running her mouth that I had a big dick. I wanted to bust out laughing when she told me, but it wasn't the right time to do some dumb shit like that. I decided to check Sierra while we were speaking.

"Yo, B, don't you ever make that mistake of pullin' a burner on me if you 'on't intend to use it," I warned.

"Nah, you betta stop playin' wit' me before I have to fuck yo' ass up," she fired back.

"Like I told you, ma. I'm not fuckin' shorty. She just cool peeps, and you ain't got nothin' to worry about."

"I'm not worried. Shit, yo' hoes need to be, though, 'cause I'm nothing nice to be fucked wit'."

I didn't respond. I couldn't do nothing but respect her gangsta. She was like the female version of me. I knew I had found my match, and we were a dangerous combo.

I decided to take her to New York to soften the tension. She often complained that she never left Virginia. We stayed at my house in the Bronx. I was happy to show her how real niggas flossed in the Big Apple.

Darryl and his chick came along for the trip, so while the ladies shopped, we handled business. He got his cousin Priscilla to show the women around. It was kind of good to see her again. I had a crush on her for the longest time, but she wasn't tryin'a give the pussy up to no dime-bag nigga. She went for the head nigga at the time; a cat named Jay from New Rochelle. The last I heard he was banging her and the whole Gun Hill Projects. Oh well, her loss.

I gave Sierra seven grand to blow. Darryl gave his girl and his cousin some paper.

"Yo, son, you really into shorty?"

"Yo, it's like she the first bitch that understand a nigga. Plus, she accept whatever I do without trippin'."

"Word? Maybe it's time we hang up our playas' robe. We getting old and shit," I said.

We went uptown and hollered at my connect. I was copping so much work he went down on his price, which was wonderful 'cause I was locking Richmond down and had spread out to Petersburg and Norfolk. Money was definitely being made.

When we got back to the Bronx, it was dark outside. The girls were chilling in the living room, smoking weed. Sierra showed me her appreciation by tonguing me down in front of everybody. I glanced over her shoulder and saw Priscilla checking me out with envy in her eyes. I knew then I was going to be tapping that ass real soon.

We sat and kicked it for a minute, reminiscing on our childhood. Before we knew it, it was midnight. We decided to call it a night 'cause everybody was beat.

Sierra Rogers

I couldn't believe that Alijah was playing me with that nasty bitch Luscious, who sucked and fucked everything that involved a dollar. He came home trying to talk to me, but fuck him. He wasn't going to keep throwing his dick around, and then think shit was sweet.

Yes, I was fucking him while he was married, but I didn't know. By time I found out, I was in too deep. I wasn't going to front; I was in love with his ass, but he wasn't going to bring another bitch into our relationship. I've been humble, patiently waiting on him to leave his fucking wife alone. I be damned before I let another ho get in.

Call me a punk, but I couldn't keep acting like I was angry with him. I went south on his ass; let him know not to ever play with me again. I was dead-ass serious. I was going to fuck him up real bad. I was getting tired of his shit already. If he didn't want me, he needed to get his ass out of the way and let the next nigga get some of my good pussy, and in return, let me live the good life.

***

I was excited we were heading to New York. I had never been out of Virginia, and I always wanted to visit the city that never slept. I thought we were going by ourselves until we stopped over by Chesterfield and picked up his boy and his girl.

Symone and I hit it off instantly. She was from the South. I usually didn't fuck with chicks from there, but she seemed cool. This was her first time out of Virginia too, so we sat back and discussed how we were going to act when we got up there.

I fell in love with New York instantly. It was everything that I imagined. We stayed at Alijah's house in the Bronx. We were tired, so we got Chinese food, smoked some good weed, and called it a night.

The next day, I got up and got dressed. I was fresh to death. I couldn't let those up top broads outdo me. Symone looked cute too. Even though she had a face only a mother could love, her body was tight, and she knew how to dress.

I didn't know what our plans were for the day, so we waited to see. As we were having breakfast, the doorbell rang. Darryl answered it. That's when a dark-skinned chick walked in. They hugged each other.

"Well, hello to you, Alijah," she said, rolling her eyes.

I didn't know who she was, so I kept my cool. I hoped she wasn't one of his flings. I hoped he wasn't playing after all the drama we just went through.

Darryl introduced her as his cousin Priscilla. We got to talking like we had known each other for a lifetime. The guys blessed us with some money, and we hit the stores. We went to Fordham Road. This was the first time that I had seen a whole bunch of stores on one strip.

We then went to the Village in Manhattan. We went crazy. This was the place that Charley had always bragged about. I saw the reason why. There were faggots parading the streets dressed in women's clothing. Symone kept pointing out a couple of bad bitches that in reality were grown-ass men. Then we went crazy in the stores. Before we knew it, it was nighttime, and we were hungry and tired.

The guys were still out, so we just kicked it, showing off our outfits to one another. Then Priscilla had some Dro, so she rolled up a fat blunt, and we smoked it. She turned out to be a cool broad. She even invited us back without the guys. Symone and I agreed.

The guys finally popped up while we were hitting the blunt. I was happy to see my boo. I jumped on him right away and kissed him. My plan was to show ownership. I had a feeling he and Priscilla had a past together.

Priscilla left, and I decided to call it a night. Alijah soon followed. We discussed our day, but he looked disturbed, like something was bothering him.

"Is everything a'ight, boo?"

"Ma, I need you to do me a favor, but you can always say no."

"What is it, boo? You know I'll do anything for you."

"Ma, I have some product that I gotta take back to Virginia, but I need a female driver for the rental car."

That's when it registered in my mind what Alijah was asking me—to drive his drugs back to Virginia.

"I can't believe you'd think that I would jeopardize myself like that. Why would you ask me some shit like that? What I look like . . . a mule?" I looked at him in disbelief.

"Ma, like I said, all you have to do is say no. I'm not forcing you to do shit. I'm tired. I'm not gonna beef wit' you." He turned his back to me, which made me angrier. I felt like crying. I didn't understand why he was treating me like that.

I tried to fall asleep, but I couldn't. All types of thoughts ran through my head. I love him, but I wasn't going to risk my freedom.

I checked the time; it was 4:00 a.m. I looked over at Alijah; he was still asleep. It was at that moment that I made the decision to drive the car for him. I asked God to watch over me while I made the worst decision of my life.

I was up and dressed before Alijah got up.

"Good morning, boo—"

He cut me off before I could finish my sentence. "Listen, ma, if it's about last night, I was dead wrong fo' askin' you some shit like that, so don't trip. I'ma handle it."

"Alijah, listen, I been up all night, and I decided to do it. I told you once before I'ma ride with you to the end."

He gave me a suspicious look. "Ma, you sure?"

"Boy, yes, I'm sure. What time we leaving?"

"I'ma wake Darryl up, then we out." He left the room.

I wondered if Symone knew about it without telling me. I wouldn't put anything past another bitch, but it was fucked up that I was left in the dark.

The ride back to Virginia, I stayed on point, looking out for the police. I maintained the speed limit and kept the music low. I saw the amount of drugs they put in the car; it'd get both me and Symone life in the penitentiary. We talked about everything, trying to get our mind off of the situation. I breathed a sigh of relief when I saw the Broad Street exit.

Shayna Jackson

I started my new job at La Blank and Associates. I was used to being the head bitch in charge, but this would do for now. I didn't plan on being there for long. As soon as I got my plan into motion and everything moves along, I would disappear in the blink of an eye.

I also retained a divorce lawyer. I was going to claim everything that was rightfully mine. I deserved every red cent for all the pain and suffering that I went through. I refused to let anything or anyone stand in the way of me and my riches.

I was seeing more of Markus too. Whenever Alijah went out of town, Markus would fill in. He told me that Alijah threatened him, but to my surprise, instead of him being scared, he was angrier that Alijah went to his house and disrespected him. Hmm . . . I liked the new and improved Markus. He finally grew a backbone. Maybe I was wrong about him being a punk.

I couldn't help but wonder what that visit was really about. I knew it was either he found out that Markus was stealing his money or that he was sleeping with his wife. Whichever one it was, I had a feeling that things were about to turn ugly real fucking soon!

I knew I had to speed up what I was doing. When I was done with Alijah, he was going to wish he had never met me. He would just be another BBNP, meaning black broke nigga in prison. I had a little something planned for his bitch too. She was going to feel my wrath intensively. All the shit she was talking about, let's see if she could do the walk.

Ha-ha! I laughed. I couldn't wait to see the look on their faces when they received their big surprise.

Chapter Twelve

Alijah Jackson

I got word where the niggas were staying at and called a meeting ASAP; no time to waste.

"We gonna ride in two cars. We gonna be in and out," I warned.

"So, how we gonna do this, Boss?" Dre asked.

"Word is they be using the back entrance that lead to Chimborazo Blvd. It's a cut back there, so we gonna park beside the church. That won't make us look suspicious; then we can run through the cut. Their escape route can become their death trap," I said, looking at my niggas. This had to be done. Before the day was over, their moms and girlfriends would be making funeral arrangements.

We split up in two cars; Darryl, Saleem, and I rode together. As we drove down Thirty-third Street to scope out the front entrance, the block was clear. We continued down to the boulevard.

It was our lucky day; the block was clear. Saleem was going to stay in the car, just in case any unwanted visitors popped up.

We got out and sprinted through the alley to the back door. Chuck, with his heavy weight, kicked the door in. It flew open, and we went in busting. They were on point, busting right back at us. We had masks over our faces, so I knew they were trying to figure out who the fuck we were.

I scoped out the nigga C-Lo. He was kneeling over one of his homies that got hit. I made eye contact with my niggas. I sneaked around the couch. He didn't even see me coming, so I walked up on him and removed my mask.

"Whaddup? I see we meet again."

"The fuck! I thought you were d-e-a-d," he stuttered and looked at me as if he'd seen a ghost.

"Nah, but you are," I said before putting one to his dome. He fell to the ground. I stood over him, and then put one between his eyes.

"That's for me, pussy."

I was enjoying the kill too much until I heard a string of shots ringing out. I ducked behind the couch while trying to analyze the situation. I heard Dre yell out, "Nahhhhhhhhhhhhhh . . ."

In the pit of my stomach, I knew one of my people got hit, but who? The fire ceased. I held my gun and headed toward the living room where all the commotion was coming from. I saw only two niggas standing, looking down. I tried to walk faster to see what they were lookin' at. My knees were wobbly, and I felt nauseated.

First, I saw the body of a nigga that I didn't recognize. When I got to what my niggas were looking at, it was Darryl's body spread across the floor with a couple of slugs to the chest. Blood gushed out of his wounds.

"Nooooooooooooo!" I dropped on my knees, picking his head up.

"C'mon, homie, stop playin' wit' me," I started to talk to him. "Get up, bruh; joke mode is ova," I said while shaking him. Tears kept rolling down like rain.

"Son, he's gone. Let's get outta here before the police come." Saleem tried to pull me up.

"Nah, son, he's not gone. It's all a joke; you'll see."

At that point, I knew I wasn't making sense, but I needed to believe that it was all a dream.

"C'mon, son, we got to go right now," he demanded.

I didn't want to leave my brother lying there like that. I took my Sean John coat off and covered him up. I knew he was cold.

Saleem pulled me out of the house, and we got in the car. As we pulled off, police sirens were heading toward the Thirty-third Street entrance. My body felt numb. I kept picturing his face. I knew it was my fault; I should'a handled business by myself.

"Yo, bro, you gon' be a'ight," Saleem assured me with his voice trembling. I knew he was hurting too.

We all got back to Sierra's house. As we walked toward the door, Dre and Chuck didn't say a word, but I knew they were fucked up inside.

Sierra must've sensed something was wrong 'cause as soon as we got in the door she ran to me. "Where is Darryl, babe?"

"Ma, he's gone. He's dead," I said before collapsing to the floor.

I woke up that night on the couch with Sierra sitting beside me.

"Baby, I made you some peppermint tea." She handed me a cup.

"Nah, ma, I need sump'n stronger. Bring me a bottle of vodka and roll me up a couple of blunts," I instructed her.

As I downed the bottle, it burned my throat, but I really didn't give a fuck. My heart was crushed. My boy, my brotha since the seventh grade, was gone. Who was going to watch my back now? Life was never going to be the same.

"Sierra, my boy is gone," I said while hugging her as tight as I could. She was all I had left.

"Baby, he's in a better place."

"Yea, yea, God should've took me instead, B. He didn't deserve that. It was *my* beef."

"Yea, you right, but Darryl was gon' ride with you, no matter what."

Before the night was over, I had finished two bottles of vodka mixed with Jamaican white rum and smoked about five blunts. It had been awhile since I got pissy drunk, but I had to block out the entire day's events. The next day was going to be even harder. I'd have to make the trip to go tell Ms. Lulu that her only son was lying in the morgue.

Sierra Rogers

The way they stormed up in the house, I knew something was wrong. They all hovered around in the kitchen. Twenty minutes later, they were out the door. As I flew downstairs, I had a weird feeling that he was about to do something off the chain. The only thing I could say was to be careful.

I could've tried stopping him, but he was a grown-ass man that was going to do whatever he chose. I whispered a silent prayer to God to protect my baby. At a time like that, I wanted to be by his side. I was no stranger to gunplay.

All I could do was smoke a blunt to calm my nerves, but that didn't help none. I kept pacing back and forth like a crackhead geeking from a good hit. Every car that I heard racing down the street, I peeked through the window, wishing to God that it was Alijah.

Minutes felt like hours. I still hadn't heard from him. Maybe I should've got in the car and went and looked for him, but where would I start? I decided just to sit tight and wait for him. I got tired of peeping through the window, so I lay on the couch. That's when I heard a car pulling up. I got up and ran to the window. I saw niggas getting out. My heart skipped a beat when I didn't see Alijah. I quickly opened the door; that's when I saw Alijah. I smiled at him, but he didn't smile back. That's when it occurred to me that something was terribly wrong. I saw everyone except Darryl. When I inquired, that's when I got the devastating news that he was dead!

Alijah fell out on the floor. I looked at the other guys for some type of explanation, but their faces said it all. I started to cry, not so much for myself, but for my man. I knew how tight they were.

I got myself together and dialed Symone's number. I knew she was going to go crazy, but I had to break the news to her before Channel 6 News did.

"Hey, gurl," she answered in a cheery voice.

I paused for a second. I hated that I had to be the bearer of bad news, so I just busted out crying.

"Sierra, what's wrong, gurl? Is it Alijah?" she asked in a concerned tone.

"*Sniff . . . sniff . . .* Symone, it's Darryl." I could barely get the words out.

"Gurl, what his crazy ass done did now? Is he there with you?"

"Symone, he's dead. He got shot earlier."

"Sierra, stop playin' like that. The joke is over; now put that nigga on the phone!"

"I'm dead-ass serious. He's dead."

"I don't believe you. He just left here 'bout two hours ago to go handle some business. Hold on while I call him on three-way. You'll see; he's alive."

I didn't respond. I knew she was in denial, and that was just her way of convincing herself he was alive. We sat on the phone while she dialed his number. The phone rang about seven times before his voice mail kicked in. I wept in silence for the fact that I wouldn't be hearing his voice again. It must've finally hit Symone because she started to holler. I heard the grief in her voice, and I couldn't take it no more.

"Symone, Symone."

Still no answer.

I hoped she didn't fall out like Alijah had. I continued holding on until she came back on the phone.

"What happened to my baby? Tell me sump'n."

"I don't know the whole story. All I know is they went 'round Church Hill, they got to shooting, and Darryl got hit up a couple of times." I kept it simple. I wasn't going to implicate my man in any of this. He could tell her exactly what happened.

We talked some more; then I hung up. I felt bad for her. They were so into each other. I felt her pain. In reality, that could've been me in her shoes.

I curled up beside my boo on the couch, thanking God it wasn't him. I cut the television on to catch the 10:00 p.m. news on CBS. There it was on the screen. The anchor lady was standing in front of a house on Thirty-third Street.

"Yes, Sam, I'm standing in front of the house where a deadly massacre happened earlier today. Five young men were found on the inside dead after neighbors alerted the police about

gunshots fired. Here goes the chief of police for the Richmond PD."

"Chief Dwyer, could you tell us anything about what happened here earlier?"

"Ms. Ross, at the moment, we're still investigating. We're looking into some promising leads, but we're pretty sure it was drug related at this time. But like I said earlier, we're still early in the investigation, and we will put all our resources to bring the person or persons responsible for this heinous crime to justice. We will not tolerate this kind of behavior in our city. Beware, whoever you are. We're coming for you," he said and pointed in the camera.

He looked straight in the camera as if he knew who he was directing his message to. I felt he had eyes that could reach all the way into my living room.

I dozed off into darkness, thinking, *Will it ever end, or is it just the beginning of more drama to come?*

Alijah Jackson

The day following Darryl's death was a standstill for me. I didn't know if I was coming or going; liquor and weed became my best friends.

Chuck went up top to handle his funeral arrangements. I should've made that trip, but truth is, I was not able to face his moms, at least not yet.

I ended up staying at the crib with Shayna. I don't know what brought me there. I just needed to be near someone who knew where we were coming from. He was the best man at our wedding. Even though he wasn't feeling Shayna, he gave me his blessing and played his position.

Sierra had been calling. At first, she caught an attitude 'bout why I was over there and not at home with her. I shut her down instantly. I wasn't feeling her coming at me sideways.

My mom called trying to convince me to come home. It was pissing me off. Everyone believed that they knew what was best for me. Well, if they knew so damn much, give me my brotha back! Darryl was a loyal partner, friend, and brotha. He was the last of a dying breed. I wanted revenge, but the niggas were all dead. I was gon' miss him. Heaven just received a soldier.

"Take care of my homie," I said, looking up to the sky, not knowing who was listening.

I got it together long enough to go check on shorty. Symone was two months pregnant with his seed, and he didn't even know. It was funny, that's all he used to joke about. It was a shame he wasn't going to be there to help raise his seed. I told her not to trip 'bout nothing; I got her. I was going to make sure they were well taken care of.

His funeral was exactly a week from the day he got killed, so I made the trip up top. A few homies volunteered to go down south and turn it upside down. I assured them everything was under control. I couldn't risk making the situation worse than what it was. Saleem already told me that the street was talking.

After I left Harlem, I made the hardest trip I ever made—to Ms. Lulu's crib. I knew she had a lot of questions and was waiting to see my face. I wasn't ready to tell her the naked truth.

"Good to see you, Alijah," she greeted me with a hug. She held me longer than she intended to.

"I know it's been awhile."

I sat down on the sofa beside her. I remembered when Darryl bought it for her after he bought her the house. He was so happy to be the first one of his six siblings that was able to buy her a crib.

"Alijah, tell me someting, anyting. What happen down dere wit' mi bwoy," she pleaded in her Trinidadian accent, tears streaming down her face.

I guess you can call me a coward, but I couldn't come out and tell her I was the reason why her son was dead. I knew they were looking for someone to blame, and I just wasn't ready. I was already dealing with my own guilt of not being there to watch his back. Instead, I was enjoying the feeling of killing dude while my brotha was getting killed.

"Aunt Lulu, we were just in the wrong place at the wrong time," I said while I rubbed her back.

"Listen to me, baby," she said and took my hand. Her hands were ice cold, and she was trembling.

"Promise me, Alijah, to leave those streets alone. I know what y'all was out there doing. His daddy lived the same life and didn't even live to see twenty-five. Instead, I had to fend fo' myself. Please, don't put yo' mama through this pain that I'm feelin' right now," she begged.

Her words broke my heart even more. I hugged her and let loose. I shed tears for my homie. We sat in silence for a little while until the doorbell rang. It was Priscilla, Darryl's younger cousin. She sashayed in and gave me a disgusted look.

"What's good with you, ma, lookin' at a nigga like you crazy?"

"Bwoy, please, where the fuck you was at when my cousin got killed?"

I wasn't going to disrespect Aunt Lulu, but as soon as she got up to answer the telephone, I dug in that ass.

"Yo, B, don't come at me like that. You know I love your cuz like a brotha. I would give my life fo' that nigga. Believe that, so stop trippin'. Yo, so when you gon' let me tap that ass?"

"I knew you were always crazy. Don't you have a wife and a bitch on the side? I'd say you have your hands full," she said, licking her lips.

"Yo, ma, it's just 'bout you and me, and since we're both grown, let's do what we been meaning to do fo' a while now," I said, grabbing my dick.

I was happy that her aunty didn't bust up in there. That gave me enough time to reel Priscilla into my trap. We eventually decided to leave and head for the Telly. Shorty gave me some head, and I beat the pussy up. It helped to relieve some of my stress. We went at it all night until we both fell out.

I gave her my cell to holla at me. I wouldn't mind fucking her on the regular. I couldn't be anything to her but a cutty buddy, 'cause even though we were like family, she was just like the rest of them hoes. Mike Jones said it best, "Back then they didn't want me; now I'm hot they all on me." She was out of luck because the only bitch I was wifeing was Sierra.

I got sharp for the funeral. It was my boy's day, and I had to represent. Sierra and Symone had already left with Priscilla. By the time I got to the church, the parking lot was full. I knew my boy had a lot of fans, but it was like the whole dope boys' fraternity was present, along with all the gangsta chicks. I knew he was looking down with pride and saying, "Damn, *I'm* the man."

I smiled and looked up to the sky and uttered, "Yea, partner, you that nigga."

I peeped niggas from Yonkers, White Plains, Harlem, and Brooklyn. When I walked up, I felt like a celebrity. People were running toward me to pay their respect. I kind of got paranoid even though I had my vest on and my nine on my waist. I peeped my fam and walked over to them. We then walked in together. I instantly peeped some DTs although they had plain clothes on, I guess trying to disguise themselves, but I could smell them a mile way.

I sat beside Mom-dukes and Aunt Lulu. Shayna was also seated beside them. I tried looking around for Sierra and Symone, but the church was so full, I didn't see them. I loved the fact that the hood was showing so much love.

The pastor finally rolled in in a cheap-ass blue suit, like he was a cheap version of Snoop

Dogg. Man, Darryl was really laughing as he looked down on this clown. He talked about my nigga like he knew him personally. He kept telling all the young thugs to put their weapons down and pick up the Bible as their sword. All due respect to the pastor, but in my world, if you got caught slipping, the Bible wasn't goin' to protect you. You needed a loaded burner. The old heads were clapping and cheering him on in agreement.

He finally ended the service. I was ready to put my man to rest. My head was pounding, and I was ready to get twisted. We had a get-together planned at a little spot on Bay Chester. It wasn't anything big, just a couple of homies celebrating the life of a soldier.

Shayna's crazy tail started some beef with Sierra before we left the church. I had to check that bitch in front of everybody, and I didn't give a fuck. I was definitely tired of that stalking-ass bitch. She liked to show her ass and didn't give a fuck. I wanted that bitch out of my life for good!

I was happy that the day was finally over. We all sat around smoking and drinking and reminiscing on the good times that we had. He was gone but not forgotten.

Sierra Rogers

I was trying my hardest to be patient, especially at a time when he was going through his boy's death. Instead of him staying home so I could really be there for him, he was over at Shayna's playing house. Nah, let me correct that; he needed "space." He needed to make his damn mind up. One second, he hated that bitch, and then the next, he was in her face.

See, I wouldn't be tripping if he had gone to one of his spots. Instead, he was laid the fuck up with this bitch. You can call me paranoid, but I felt like he wanted to have his cake and eat it too. I'd tried talking to him, but the end result was always the same. This nigga got fucking nerves calling *me* selfish.

Let's get on the topic. I'd been faithful the entire time that we had been kicking it, while he railroaded me into believing that he was a single man; but truth was, he belonged to another bitch. Even though he didn't man up 'bout Luscious, he wasn't just chilling with her for no fucking conversation. Since he wanted to play games, he could do that on the next bitch's time.

I turned my attention back to running my shop. I didn't know it was so hectic when you ran your own joint. I'd also become Symone's caretaker. She took dude's death real hard. It was even harder because she was knocked up and didn't even get a chance to let him know.

Me and Mo' rallied around taking care of her, but our presence didn't make a difference. She was falling deeper and deeper into depression. One time she swore that Darryl was rubbing her stomach. I had to shake her numerous times to get her out of her trance and back into reality.

We had to force her to eat. If not for herself, she had to do it for her baby's sake. But she turned out luckier than other bitches in the same situation. Before Darryl died, he bought her a house and a brand-new car and left over two hundred thousand in a safe.

The dummy was talking about she was going to bring it to his mom. I corrected her real fast. What they didn't know wasn't going to hurt them. Plus, times was too hard out there, especially for a young black female knocked up without a baby daddy. Unless she wanted to go join the long line waiting on government money the first of the month, she better quit talking crazy and come to her senses real fast.

Symone wasn't too eager to go the funeral. She hadn't met any of his family except for Priscilla, and I really hoped his mother was nothing like Alijah's mom. I was tired of preaching to her, but she was my girl, and I wanted her to have a backbone. It was too late for her to be scared. Either his family accepted her and the baby, or it was their loss. A bitch of my caliber wouldn't give a fuck. I would've told them motherfuckas to kiss my black ass real fast without giving it a thought.

I decided to go to the funeral with her even though I knew Shayna was going to be there, but fuck that bitch. I had to be there for my bitch. I drove to New York. I loved being up there, but the traffic was tighter than a sealed window. Yellow Cabs were all over the place like they owned the damn streets.

Priscilla invited us to stay with her, but I turned it down. Shorty was cool peoples and all, but until I found out for a fact that she and Alijah were nothing but friends, I wouldn't get down like that with her. Bitches from New York were grimy just like the niggas. I be damned if I let a bitch play me close to get closer to my man.

We found a motel on Bay Chester Avenue. It wasn't no Holiday Inn, but it was clean enough to stay at for the night. We decided just get one room with double beds. Me and Mo' shared a bed, and Symone took the other one. It felt good just chilling with the girls; something I missed doing with Neisha.

We got settled in. It had been a long day. I was not only physically drained, but also emotionally. My personal life was weighing down on me. I tried to hide my feelings from the girls, but I was tearing up on the inside. I hadn't spoken to Alijah since he left Richmond two days earlier. I tried calling his phone but got no answer. I was going to give him the business after Darryl got buried because I was fucking tired of his bullshit!

Alijah finally called to see where we were. We drove to his house before we left for the church.

I brought me a black Vera Wang minidress and a black pair of Jimmy Choo pumps. Li'l Mo' hooked my hair up with a twenty piece sewn in. Instead of going to a funeral, I should be on my way to a photo shoot overseas. Lol.

Mo' had on a long Versace dress that generously hugged her curves, and her hair was pinned up in a Chinese bun. Symone wore a black pinstriped pantsuit. I hooked her hair up on a simple but cute flat twist with a curly ponytail. If you asked me, we looked damn good!

When we got to the church, the line of cars went as far back as two blocks long. The one-way street was turned into a roadblock. We sat waiting to get in. By the looks of things, one would've thought that T.I. or Young Jeezy was in the house. I been to a lot of funerals, unfortunately, but those up north folks were getting their shine on.

Symone started to bawl as soon as we stepped foot in the door. I felt like crying too, but I kept it together for my girl. Mo' took her to go view his body; I couldn't face him. I didn't want to remember him lying in a casket, and I was not good at saying good-bye.

The ceremony was long and drawn out. I had a feeling the pastor was paid for his performance. He was behaving like he was geeked up. The people felt him, though. Every statement that he started, they ended it with "amen." Outbursts were heard throughout the church. Darryl was truly missed.

When it finally ended, that's when I spotted Alijah. He was standing with his mom and who I assumed was Darryl's mom, and none other than Shayna. Mo' must've spotted them too.

"Let's go, Sierra. Don't study that," she said, pulling my arm.

The crowd was stagnant. Everyone was trying to pay their respects to the family. From what I saw, he had a big family. I saw Shayna pushing through the crowd coming toward me. I braced myself for the drama that was getting ready to kick off.

"Well well well, if it isn't the bitch that broke my marriage up. What the hell are you doing here?" she said, looking me up and down.

"Well well well, if it isn't the wretch whose husband loves making love to *meeee*. I'm here to pay my respect to Darryl and support my man."

"Well, you're not welcome here. He's still *my* husband, and by the looks of it, he's here with *me*."

I took a step closer. "Listen, bitch! I'ma ask you to get outta my fuckin' face before I forget where the fuck I am and tear your ass up in here," I said and balled up my fist.

"This is not over by a long shot," she said and strolled off into the crowd.

"Count on it, bitch. I got you the next time we meet," I yelled, not giving a fuck who heard, and by the looks, everyone did. "Gurl, do you believe that bitch just stepped to me?" I asked in disbelief.

"Don't pay that miserable bitch no mind. Let her have him." Symone's ass blurted out that dumb-ass shit.

I wasn't going to hold that against her; she wasn't in her right frame of mind.

"Fuck that, Sierra. I 'on't wanna be all up in yo' B.I., but I'm ready to beat that bitch ass my damn self," Mo' said.

Alijah must've spotted what went down, because when I looked back, he was all in her face yelling. I couldn't hear what he was saying, but I knew he was checking that bitch.

"C'mon, y'all, let's get this over with."

We walked into the cold air. It was only November, but it felt like mid-February. We forgot to take our coats, trying to look cute and all, and we were freezing our ass off.

The cemetery was more crowded than the church. We couldn't get close to the casket. Symone was back on her routine, crying and shaking. A few hood buggers rolled by and rolled their eyes at us. They must be some of Darryl's fans. They hated on Symone and kept it moving. They must have sensed trouble was in the air. I didn't give a fuck if we were on their turf and outnumbered. I was already pissed and was ready to pounce on anyone who stood in my fucking path.

After the funeral, we went to a get-together they had for him. Symone got to meet his family, and it turned out well. His mom was happy to know she had a grandbaby on the way.

Alijah and I talked, argued, then fucked. So much for being mad at him.

Shayna Jackson

Markus was always the bearer of bad news. He called me and told me that Darryl was killed. He could've saved that call. I could care less about any of Alijah's sidekicks. Plus, me and Darryl never saw eye to eye from day one. I personally thought he was trying to be too much like Alijah. I even told him that I didn't trust his boy and his motives. Instead, he turned it around on me saying that I was jealous of the bond they shared.

Darryl was nothing but a womanizer. They said birds of a kind flocked together; no wonder Alijah became a whore. I wouldn't be shocked if it was a bitter woman or some woman's husband killed his ass.

I called Alijah's phone to express my condolences, but his voice mail came on. In a time like that, a husband needed his wife. God worked in a mischievous way because when I got home, Alijah was there in our bed asleep. It was so funny because he was lying on the same sheets I fucked Markus's brains out on earlier that morning. It didn't matter. What he didn't know wasn't going to hurt him. That was a close call, though. I didn't expect him to come home.

I took a shower and got in bed beside him, hugging him closely. He returned the gesture. For the night, we both blocked the outside world out and found comfort in each other's arms.

His phone kept ringing nonstop. I glanced at the ID, and it was from an unknown caller. Hmm . . . Somebody must be feeling lonely on that cold winter night. I smiled and rolled back over.

In the morning, I got up and cooked breakfast: pancakes, eggs, and sausage with grits. I set the table and waited for Alijah to wake up. His eyes were bloodshot red. The last time that I saw him in that state was when I lost our baby.

"I heard what happened to Darryl." I stretched out my arm and touched his arm.

"Yea, ma, my nigga gone."

I got up and walked over to him and rubbed his back. "He's in a better place. God knows what's best for us," I said while rolling my eyes behind his back.

We talked for about an hour. I listened to him as he reminisced about their time together, the women that they shared, murders they committed together. Things couldn't get any better than that. *Good things definitely come to those that wait,* I thought.

Alijah was so busy diving into self-pity that he never noticed that I was sitting beside him with a minitape recorder. *Got you!* I smiled and walked off.

I drove up to New York for the funeral. I wouldn't have missed it for the world. I bought me a nice cocktail dress for the occasion. I guessed I was the only one that was celebrating. I got me a hotel room at the Hilton in White Plains. I didn't feel like staying at my mother-in-law's house. I had to start distancing myself, because when all hell broke loose, I wanted no attachments.

Later on, I drove out to Long Island. I hadn't seen my parents in a while, not since we fell out over Alijah. I missed my mom, but more so my daddy. I'd always been Daddy's little girl. At times, my mom would get jealous at all the attention that he showed me. I was hoping that our marriage would turn out like my parents', but as I found out, Alijah was nothing like my father. He couldn't walk a day in my father's shoes.

As I pulled up to the mansion that I grew up in, I felt nervous to face my folks, especially Daddy. Our conversation was always the same . . . *"Sugar, when are you going to leave that drug-dealing boyfriend of yours and come on back home?"*

I would reply, *"Daddy, he's not a drug dealer. He's a legitimate businessman who happens to be your son-in-law."*

He would drop the subject just to bring it back up later. I kept ringing the doorbell, but no one answered. I dialed both their numbers, and their voice mails came on. I waited about five minutes; then I walked to the neighbor's house. He had been our neighbor since we moved there. He was nosy as hell, so he should know where they were. I rang his doorbell. He looked confused when he opened the door.

"Hello, it's me, Shayna."

"Oh yes, yes, you so grown up. I didn't recognize you." He stared at my chest like he'd never seen breasts before. He had always been an old pervert.

"Well, sorry to disturb you. I was looking for my parents, but they're not home. Do you have any idea where they could be?"

"They didn't tell you they'd be on a three-week cruise across the Caribbean?"

"No, I haven't talked to them in a while. I should've called first. Anyway, thank you. I have to get going."

"Are you sure? You're welcome to come in. We could do some catching up on old memories and even make a few new ones of our own." He looked at me while batting his eyelashes.

"I'm pretty sure that I have better things to do than spend my evening with a dirty old man like you." I stormed off feeling disappointed. I was looking forward to spending some time with my parents.

By the time I got back to my hotel, I was even more disappointed. I soaked in some bubble bath and sipped on a glass of Chardonnay. I closed my eyes and took a deep breath. *Tomorrow is going to be a great day*, I thought. A lot of bitches that my husband fooled around with would be showing their faces, but most important, that bitch Sierra was going to be there.

I got in the bed around 11:00 p.m. I tried to call Alijah. I got no answer, so I called his mom. She hadn't seen him either. Hmm . . . His cheating ass could be anywhere shacked up with one of his bimbos.

I got up bright and early and called Alijah. "So, where you was at last night?" I waited for him to tell a big fat lie, like he was at his mom's house.

"Yo, ma, it's too early to start naggin'. I'ma grown-ass man; don't question me."

"You're a *married* man too. You just don't sleep wherever the fuck you choose to."

"Listen, B, don't keep reminding me that I'm married to a psychotic bitch."

His lame ass hung up in my face.

"Bastard! You are going to pay dearly," I yelled at him, even though he was long gone.

I was fascinated by the size of the funeral. This was my first drug-dealer funeral. They lived large and went out large. Fashion Day in the Big A was the way to describe the atmosphere. The police would have gotten a fat bonus from the mayor because I was sure they would have made some good money from illegal parking to illegal guns and drugs—you name it. I would've done well too; picked up some new clients, just like old times.

The ceremony was long and boring. I could've stayed home or went shopping. It was crazy how when a person was living they were the worst, but as soon as they kicked the bucket, they were the most wonderful person in the world. When I croak, they can just cremate my ass because I don't want no fake-ass pastor yelling over my damn body.

I felt weird having all those people around me crying. Most of them were faking, and they didn't really miss him. They were crying over his money. I just hoped his mother was smart enough to take out life insurance on him. She knew that her son was living recklessly, and that's why I had a million dollars on Alijah's head. With all the money he had, I was going to be one rich bitch—make that *Ms. Rich Bitch!*

After the charade was over, I saw the bitch standing with all her friends. I walked up on her and two other project-looking bitches. I let her ass know that she wasn't welcome. That bitch made my skin crawl. It was just something about her ass; I just couldn't pinpoint it as of yet. I would've dug into her ass if I wasn't looking so cute, but there's a time and place for everything. When the bitch threatened me, I had murder on my mind. I would love to see her face when a slug from my nine millimeter hits her in the head.

I walked back over to Alijah so I could return to playing my position as the doting wife. When I tried to hold on to him, he snatched his arm away.

"What tha fuck you in Sierra face fo'? You 'on't know how to fuckin' act, B."

"What are you talking 'bout? I just said hello to her. Any friend of yours is a friend of mine."

"Whateva, bitch! When we get back to Virginia, I'm done with yo' ass. Better yet, why don't you stay up here with yo' peoples? Make yo' daddy proud; stay the fuck away from me."

"Alijah, baby, calm down. It's not that serious," I said, looking around to make sure none of the haters were listening.

"Bitch, get tha fuck outta my face. Yo, how 'bout you leave right now? Darryl wouldn't want yo' ass here anyway."

I couldn't believe that he was talking to me like that, all because I stepped to his whore. Baby boy had the game twisted. No one talks to me like that and gets away with it. It wouldn't be a bad idea for me to stay in New York, but I had big plans in Richmond, Virginia.

As I walked off to go mingle, I was so furious I wanted to scream, but I brushed my shoulders off, kissed my mother-in-law good-bye, and headed back down South.

Chapter Thirteen

Alijah Jackson

I was back on the grind, still had a business to run. I kept a low profile. My homies handled any face-to-face that took place. I also brought back my longtime brethren Dread, a thoroughbred fresh from Jamaica. He also was a stone-cold killer who was trained with JDF. He was a trained sniper. I'd seen his work firsthand, so I needed him on my team.

Sierra was showing her ass off like she wanted me to smack some sense into her so she could quit tripping. I never understood how females act so good when you first meet them, but soon after you fuck them, they switch up the game.

I also got word that I was on Richmond's most wanted, and not by the jakes, but by Creighton niggas looking to avenge their boys' deaths. See, them little niggas didn't learn a damn thing.

They weren't ready to go to war against me. I was ready to wipe the whole hood out: kids, mamas—everybody had to go.

I switched up my cars and went through the hood several times just scoping out the scene. They didn't even see me. Again, I caught them slipping.

I decided to holla at Sierra. A lot had been on my mind lately. I wasn't feeling her hanging out with Li'l Mo's chickenhead ass. I bet that I could've fucked her if I wanted to, but I wouldn't even cross that path. She looked like the type that couldn't keep her mouth shut.

"Lemme rap wit' you," I said and signaled Sierra to sit down.

"I'm busy. I got to get in the shower so I can meet up with Symone and Mo'. It's girls' night out," she said with a stupid look on her face.

"Yo, B, sit the fuck down and shut up. I been laid back while you run around here like a chicken wit' its head cut off, but this is important, so you going to listen whether or not you like it. Yo, B, you know the whole situation, so you know I'm hot right now. With that said, I have to be able to trust the people that's around me 100 percent."

I paused and looked her dead in the eyes to make sure she understood the seriousness of what I was saying; then I continued. "I know you grew up with these niggas, and y'all got history together, but that's exactly what it is . . . *history*. So, right now, I need to know who you ridin' wit'?"

"Alijah, what you tryin'a say—I'm not loyal?"

"B, I'm saying, are you down for me or not?"

"I love you; of course, I'm wit' you. What the fuck I look like . . . a fucking snake? I know what's going on with y'all, but I know where my loyalty lies," she said, tears rolling down her cheeks.

"That's what a nigga need to know. I'm not sleeping with the enemy. Ma, I need you to be cautious of your surroundings at all times. Whenever you comin' to the house, make sure you circle the block at least two times; make sure you are not being followed."

I knew if niggas couldn't get to me, they'd use her as bait. I couldn't risk that happening. I knew shorty was hurting that she had to choose between her homeboys and me, but in the streets, you can only be loyal to one. In my mind, I kind of felt guilty, because the whole time I was testing shorty, if she had shown any signs of weakness, I would've put her to sleep forever. In my world, it's death before dishonor, and loyalty was everything.

I was going over my statements that Markus brought over. I wasn't no Wall Street-type nigga, but I was good at math, especially adding numbers. I looked over my statement for the past year, and the result I kept gettin': my money kept coming up short *every single month*. Over ten grand was missing every month. It was unbelievable that snake-ass nigga was stealing right under my nose. Now I fully understood why his ass was acting weird when I paid him that visit the other day.

I rubbed my hand over my face. "Oh God, oh my, oh my," I said. I just lost one homie, and now I had to take the life of another. I wished there was another way out, but holmes been violating me right under my nose.

I went directly to Saleem. I hadn't seen much of him since I came back. We sat down and kicked it.

"Whaddup, bro?"

"Peace, my brotha." He gave dap.

"How you been holding up?"

"I'm livin', just lying low, tryin'a stay alive," I said.

"Good to see you in a better frame of mind."

"Listen, I'm just passing through, but I need to holla at you 'bout some shit I found out."

"Speak to me, brotha."

"Yo, 'member when I told you holmes was acting strange? Well, I found out why. He's been fuckin' with my paper."

"What?"

"Yea, I'm pretty sure. He the only one that handle my money."

"You confront him yet?"

"Nah, I'ma kill him."

"Mmm, handle yo' business."

"I got it, but I'ma need yo' cleanup crew."

"A'ight. Just lemme know when and where, and I'ma handle this one personally."

"Now that's settled, I'ma be outta the country fo' a week. I'ma need you to keep niggas under control."

"Word, business or pleasure?"

"A little pleasure. Wanna take Sierra to Jamaica. We been going through a lot lately. I'ma treat her to a week in the sun."

"When you leaving?"

"This weekend."

"A'ight, brotha, enjoy your trip."

"A'ight, bro, one."

I stopped by my travel agent and picked up two round-trip tickets to Kingston, Jamaica. It was Thanksgiving weekend, so niggas were getting ready to get their party on. I had everything under control. My niggas were on point, and I was ready to go.

I stopped by Shayna's house to grab a few items I had left over there. I was happy that she was not there. I didn't want to hear her mouth or see the sight of her, not after the way she behaved in New York.

Something strange hit me when I entered the bedroom. A scent hit my nose. I stood for a minute, trying to analyze the situation. It wasn't a female scent . . . That was Fahrenheit Cologne for men. I'd never used it before, so it was weird that the room was drowning with it.

I walked over to the messed up bed and smelled the sheets. They were covered with the same scent. I knew that unless Shayna had started to use men's cologne all of a sudden, it was definitely a nigga that was laid up in the sheets in my muthafuckin' bed!

I hit the door to release some frustration. Whoever that nigga was, he was one bold muthafucka coming up in my crib. Whenever I find out who it was, they were both going to be dead. That sneaky-ass bitch kept stressing me about Sierra, and all along, her trifling ass was fucking someone. She was going to regret that she ever met me.

Sierra Rogers

I was happy to be back home. Even though I liked New York, Richmond was my home. I was getting tired of all the up-and-down dealing with Symone's nervous breakdown. I was definitely drained. I felt pity for her.

A few days after the funeral, Mo' went and checked on her and found her passed out on the kitchen floor, overdosed on a bottle of Percocet. Thank God for Mo' who got her to the hospital just in time to get her stomach pumped.

I rushed over to Community Hospital after I got the news. I was happy that the doctors acted fast and saved her and the baby's life. It was out of our hands after that point. The hospital called the psych for her and had her on suicide watch.

I heard my phone ringing and dug into my pocketbook to get it. I hoped it was Alijah, but when I looked at the number, I didn't recognize it.

"Hello," I answered.

"Hey, bitch," Neisha answered.

"I didn't know you remembered this number," I said sarcastically.

"Bitch, stop trippin'. Where you at? I need to talk to you," she said with urgency in her voice.

Against my better judgment, I gave her my address.

"I be right over."

"Yeah, whatever," I said with an attitude.

I wasn't really up for company, but I wanted to know what she had been up to lately and why she'd been acting all funny toward me. I got up and brushed my teeth, washed my face, and made me a cup of hot chocolate.

Soon, I heard a car pull up. I was surprised the bitch finally got her a car. When I opened the door, I barely recognized the person that was walking toward me. She had lost a lot of weight, and her weave looked like an old map. She had bags underneath her eyes like she had been up for days. She looked like a crackhead that had been on a crack binge.

"Hey, gurl." She tried to hug me.

I gave her a slight hug, still in shock over her appearance. "Come in, it's cold out here."

She stepped inside of the house and looked on with amazement. "Damn, bitch, *this* how you living?"

"Yup, this how the queen living," I bragged.

Even though I was happy to see her, I was still upset with her. I had been calling her, and not one time did she return my call. I wondered why, all of a sudden, she decided to show her face.

"Yo, Neisha, cut the small talk. What's up? You sounded like it was important on the phone."

"Sierra, it's like that; I can't kick it wit' my bitch no more."

I didn't respond. I might be tripping, but I felt a negative vibe coming off that bitch.

"A'ight, Sierra, since you actin' all stuck up and shit, lemme get to the point. You know Li'l Tony, C-Lo, and his boys are dead."

"All right, he had it coming. You know how they get down," I said, shrugging my shoulders.

"Damn, bitch, you *did* change. You acting like you don't care."

"What! I never said I don't care. Don't put words in my mouth. Listen, stop beating around the bush. What are you trying to say? Get to the fucking point," I warned in a fierce tone.

"Sierra, you know that New York nigga you fuckin' with killed him. Don't play dumb. You need to leave that nigga alone. You 'on't wanna get caught up in that bullshit. You know the Creighton boys gon' get him and whoever else that's in the way."

"Listen, Neisha, whoever the fuck sent you to deliver their message, fuck them, and before you start running around here being a flunky, get your facts straight."

"Bitch, I 'on't kno' why you getting offended. I know the nigga was lacing you, but you need to think about your life. You grew up wit' us, and you just met him. Furthermore, you defending a dude who is playing you behind your back. You stupid if you think he's only fucking you and his wife. Bitch, please!"

I was fucking hot! That bitch was up in my shit talking like that. I was about to forget that we were friends and beat the life out of her.

"Listen up, bitch, I don't give a fuck about you or them fucking niggas that you rep. My loyalty is with my man. Now get tha fuck outta my house before I whup yo' ass." I stared her down with venom in my eyes.

"I'll leave now, Ms. High and Mighty, but not long ago, you was just another broke-ass bitch fuckin' these same niggas fo' their paper. You can move a ho out of the ghetto, but you can't get the ghetto outta them."

I jumped on that heifer and started to choke her.

"Sierra, stop! Get off of me."

I didn't let up any. I continued to choke her until she started to cough. Then I eased my hands off her throat. She kept coughing with tears in her eyes.

"You fucking crazy. You gon' get yours." She got up and straightened her clothing.

"Yo, get the fuck out," I said, pushing her out the door.

After she stumbled outside, I slammed my door; then I leaned on it and started to cry. I didn't know what I was feeling. I had been nothing but good to that bitch, but what she did was betray me for some niggas that didn't even give a fuck about her. I felt crazy after I finished crying.

I called Mo'. I needed to vent a little, and she was coming through with some weed, exactly what I needed. I took a shower and put some pajamas on. I looked in the mirror. My hair was a hot mess, and I needed to get it fixed ASAP.

That brought my focus back on Neisha. What was really going on with her? She didn't look right. She was supposed to be in her last semester at VCU; life couldn't be that bad. She'd always kept her looks up. I really hoped she wasn't fucking with any drugs. I knew she loved her weed, but her deranged behavior reminded me of my mom. Neisha was always a follower; who knows what she done got herself into.

Mo' showed up with steamed shrimp, my favorite dish.

"Bitch, you just made my day."

"I figured you were starved."

"Bitch, what would I do without you?"

"Lose your mind like Symone."

We both busted out laughing.

"You stupid. How the chick doing anyways?"

"She doing better. The psych evaluated her; she should know something soon."

"I'm glad she's doing better—for her and the baby's sake."

"Enough 'bout that; let's smoke some of dis good ganja," I said, imitating Alijah's accent.

I watched as she took small drags from the fat Philly blunt.

"This some good shit here. I need to move to Jamaica, where I heard the shit is legal. I'd walk around butt-ass naked with a blunt in my hand. I'd even convert to Rastafarian."

"Pass that, you psycho bitch." I took the blunt from her.

"What you have to drink?"

"Juice or liquor, you kno' I 'on't drink soda."

"Bitch, I want some liquor."

"Well, let's see what Alijah got: Patrón, Henney, vodka, and some Jamaican white rum. You know I'm a lady, so I stick with the minor stuff—" Before I could finish my sentence that heifer cut me off.

"Get to the fucking point, Sierra."

"Hpnotiq, Alizé, or some Baileys?"

"Baileys is cool."

For the next hour, we talked about men, sex, and money. The whole time we kept laughing—more like geeking off the power of the herb. I felt like I was in heaven. It's crazy how drugs and alcohol always put me in the right mood.

I started to feel horny. Damn, I wished that Alijah was home. I was ready to spread-eagle and get fucked. When the whole bottle of liquor was gone, we started on a bottle of Alizé. We knew damn well it wasn't good to have mixed our liquor. I didn't know how it happened, but from that point on, I wasn't in control of my actions. Mr. Alizé/Baileys and Mr. Marijuana were in the driver's seat. I was a mere passenger enjoying the wild ride of ecstasy.

Sitting in front of me, Mo' was looking sexy, and I meant it in every way sexual. Now you see, I've never looked at another female like that before. I'm even scared to get undressed in front of another woman, but there I was looking at my BFF, thinking of things that I could do to her. I saw her looking right back at me with lust in her eyes.

"What you looking at, Mo'?" I startled her.

"The same thing that you was looking at a minute ago," she answered.

From that moment on, we started to kiss. Gosh! It felt so good kissing my friend. I wasn't sure what else I should be doing, but Mo' started to rub on my breast. I loved every bit of the feeling. My body responded to the alert like I wasn't new to the situation. I had plenty of niggas fondle me before, but I never reached the height of excitement as when Mo' touched me.

She continued kissing on my body, giving me full attention to each little area. I lay on the sofa enjoying the other side of sexual pleasure. She licked all the way down between my legs. She gently parted my legs and put her cute little face between my Garden of Eden. When her tongue touched my clit, it was like a magnet attached to a metal. I screamed out in agony.

Two women in bed, in most people's eyes, was a deadly sin, but in my eyes, it was the best feeling I'd ever experienced. Mo' was a pro at satisfying my pussy. She was very gentle. I never thought that I could enjoy sex without a dick, but with her razor tongue and her two fingers in me, I had multiple orgasms. When it was over, I craved for more. I even imagined returning the favor. I never thought about being a carpet muncher, but all that changed.

After we were finished, I went to the bathroom and cleaned myself off. She did the same. The silence after that was long and drawn out, an unavoidable situation. I felt a little guilty that I cheated on Alijah. I wondered what he would have done if he had walked in on us. Most guys would love to watch two chicks together, but I was scared how he might react. I decided to break the silence.

"I never knew you were a lesbian."

"A lesbian?" She looked confused, then continued. "Nah, I'm not a lesbian. I just enjoy the best of both worlds."

"So, you been with a woman before; you seemed experienced."

"You're too cute. Yea, I been with a chick before."

"Hmm. So, you sleep with your friends?"

"Sierra, what's good with all the questions? I didn't do nothing that you didn't ask for, so cut the bullshit out. You're just feeling confused 'cause it's yo' first time."

"I'm not saying that. I'm just shocked that I slept with my bestie."

"Stop saying you slept with me; all I did was ate your pussy. If it make you feel any better, a lot of chicks are doing each other, and they keep it on the low low."

"Wow! It's cool. I just don't want our relationship to change, and you can't tell it to anyone. I mean it, Mo', not even Symone. Shorty a'ight, but I don't want her in my business like that."

"You got that. Your secret is cool wit' me, boo," she said and threw a pillow at me.

We had a pillow fight, which helped to erase the tension in the air. After we were done, I went and got the air freshener and sprayed the living room. I had to get rid of the aroma of pussy that filled the air.

Alijah was tripping, so I totally avoided him. I got it on with Mo' every chance we got. We grew closer, but she knew I loved dick and wasn't going to give that up for no pussy.

Symone got out of the hospital and was feeling much better. Her mom moved in with her to keep an eye on her. I also hadn't heard from Neisha since I whupped that ass. I didn't tell Alijah about her visit, because even though I would never rock with her like that again, I still didn't want to see no harm go her way.

Alijah was home early. I noticed he had a woozy look on his face when I entered the living room. I knew something was up. He wanted to talk, but I was getting ready to take a shower so I could go hang out with Mo'. For some reason, every time I mentioned her name, he'd give me a disgusted look. I really didn't care if he liked her or not. I did, and that's all that mattered.

I looked down at the carpet. I couldn't make eye contact with him. I hated the fact that I was lying to him. I just wanted to blurt out, "I'm sleeping with Mo'," but that would've just made matters worse. I couldn't chance that. We weren't just fucking buddies. We were best friends and business partners.

We had a long conversation about loyalty. He wanted to know that I was riding with him. I felt like he had doubts about me being loyal. I assured him that I was his Bottom Bitch. I felt none of that bullshit that was going on. I wished that I could've just left and went down South to Atlanta or Florida. Sometimes I blamed the up top niggas. If they didn't have the mentality of coming to Virginia trying to run shit and put niggas down there out of business, they wouldn't have the problems they did. It was only fair, and it was enough smokers to have kept everybody in business. I was only sad that my boo got caught up in the hype.

Chapter Fourteen

Alijah Jackson

That stupid bitch Shayna thought I was stupid when I confronted her 'bout having a nigga up in my crib.

"Alijah, what are you talking about?"

"Bitch, don't play stupid. Whose cologne was that?"

"Baby, it must be yours. You have all different kinds."

"You stupid bitch, I'm not yo' baby, and I 'on't wear no cheap-ass Fahrenheit Cologne," I yelled in her face. "Yo, I should beat yo' ass right now, but I'ma do better than that. I'ma leave yo' crazy ass alone fo' good."

"Alijah, I swear to God, I never cheated on you." She started to cry.

The hatred that I felt for that bitch at that moment, I could've just blown her brains out with my nine.

"Shayna, be a fuckin' woman. Who the nigga you had up in here?" I shook that bitch as if she were a rag doll. She didn't respond, just kept crying. "You wanna know sump'n? I should'a left yo' conniving ass when you lost my seed. Instead, I let you stay around, took care of yo' ass, but you never fuckin' satisfied. I fuckin' hate you, bitch. You hear me? I fuckin' *hate* you!"

"Alijah, calm down, baby. You don't mean that; you're just upset. I'll tell you who it is if you promise me you won't leave."

I turned around and slapped that bitch so hard she fell to the ground. She lay there crying. Her tears didn't mean shit to me as I looked at her and saw her for the snake that she really was. All she did was drain me all those years. I should have listened to my boys when they tried to warn me about that trick.

I went in the bedroom and grabbed everything that was left in the closet that belonged to me. That's when she made the mistake of coming in there.

"Alijah, please don't do this to me. Don't."

I looked her dead in the eyes. "Spit it out, bitch."

"It's Markus. He's been forcing me to sleep with him."

"Who the fuck you just said?" I couldn't believe my ears.

"I said it's Markus, but I don't love him."

I stepped closer to that bitch and slapped her about ten times back-to-back. "You dirty bitch! You been fuckin' my boy! How long you been fuckin', Shayna?"

She must've sensed that I was homicidal at that point.

"Almost two years." She wept.

At that point, I punched that bitch to the floor, then hawked some cold up and spit on that bitch.

"Alijah, help me. You just broke my jaw. Please, Alijah."

"Fuck you, bitch. Why don't you just fucking die?"

I stormed out of the crib, got in my ride, and reversed. Doing damn near a 100 mph, I headed toward the city.

I saw his car outside, so I knew he was there. I made sure that no one was outside. It was dark out anyways. I saw when he peeped through his screen door.

"Yo, it's me, partna. Open up." I gave him a fake grin, and like a fool, he opened the door.

"Boss, everything a'ight?"

I looked at him as he locked the door behind us; then I pulled my gun.

"Nah, pussy, ain't shit sweet."

"Yo, Boss, what's going on?" he asked with a puzzled look on his face.

"Sit yo' bumbo claat down. I'ma get straight to the point. First, I found out you stealing my bread. Then I found out you fucking my bitch."

"What you talkin' bout, man? You mistaken. I never took a dollar from you, and I'm not fuckin' yo' bitch. I don't even like Shayna; she not my type, Boss."

The clown just tripped himself up. I never mentioned what bitch I was talkin' 'bout. By then, I knew I was going to kill him.

"Yo, B, where yo' safe at?"

"Safe?"

"Yea, pussy, yo' safe," I said, pointing my Glock at his forehead.

"It's right in the closet in the master bedroom."

"C'mon, nigga, get it." I held the gun pointed at his dome in case he had any ideas. "Open, B!" I yelled.

He was acting all nervous. It took three turns before he got it opened. I knew it wasn't half the money he took from me, but I was satisfied.

"Alijah, listen up, man, I 'on't kno' what Shayna done told you, but that bitch is lying. She just tryin'a come between our friendship. We're like brothers, man; we go way back, homie."

I was getting tired of hearing his bitch ass crying. I was going to leave him with a little dignity.

"One more thing, holmes."

"What, Boss, anything."

"Tell my dawg I said whaddup."

"Who?"

"Darryl," I said before I pulled the trigger.

His marrow flew everywhere. A few spots of blood flew on my new Air Force Ones. I got out my rag and wiped the doorknobs, took my money, and left. I eased out of the driveway into the light flow of traffic.

It was crazy how the more I killed, the easier it got for me. I remembered the first time I merked a nigga. I was fifteen. I was all shook up after I pulled the trigger, but Darryl took the gun from me and convinced me dude was going to kill me if I didn't shoot him first.

I called Saleem to let him know what was up; then I went home to spend some quality time with Sierra.

Sierra Rogers

I wasn't going to front, I was feeling like R. Kelly—the best of both worlds. After Mo' would eat my pussy, I would go home so Alijah could beat it up. Mo' made a suggestion for me to let her hit me with a strap-on dildo. I turned that down. Hell, nah! I would let her continue to eat me up, but I didn't want no fake dick when I had a big, black cock at home. She quickly dropped the subject.

At work, I tried my best not to let anyone catch on. I was surprised that no one noticed the chemistry between us.

I hadn't talked to Symone in a few days. For real, I was in my feelings because Alijah was going over to her house a little too much. I went deranged when I called him one day, and he was on his way to take her to her doctor's visit. You can call me a selfish bitch, but it is what it is. I didn't mind him checking on her because I knew he was doing his boy a favor, but I felt like that bitch was getting a little bit too comfortable with my man.

I pulled him up on it, and he assured me that nothing was going to jump off. I kind of believed him because of his loyalty to Darryl. I felt like Symone was unknowingly trying to replace her man with mines.

Thanksgiving was three days away, and I noticed that my shop was only packed with my South Side clientele; not one East End client, and they didn't even bother to cancel their appointments. It was as if someone was throwing salt on my name. I already knew it was those Creighton niggas. Now that Li'l Tony was dead, his right-hand man, Corey, took over.

I couldn't believe those fools were playing around with my money. I'd come too far for those dudes to be on some grimy shit like that. I was going to call Charley to see what the word was. I also knew that bitch Neisha was in on it.

Later that evening, Alijah picked me up from the shop. I ran into his arms like I hadn't seen him in years. I just wanted to feel his touch. No matter how fucked up my day was, whenever I got around him, it was like nothing else mattered. I never knew a man could make love not just to my body but also my mind.

"Baby, I'm happy you are here." I jumped on him.

"Damn, girl, you a'ight?"

"Yup, I'm just happy to see you."

"Word, that's what's up. Let's go then."

"Let's go."

He pulled off and then cut the music off. "So, you gonna tell me what's really goin' on?"

I busted out crying.

"Ma, what's the matter? Talk to me."

"You know all my clients from the East End didn't show up at all this week."

"So they had other plans. Why you trippin'?"

"Whatever, Alijah, I been doing their hair for years now. If they can't make it, they *always* call me to reschedule," I yelled.

"Calm down, ma. I'm just as confused as you are." He took my hand into his.

"I know they got something to do wit' it."

"They who? What are you talking 'bout? Somebody fucking with you?"

"Nah, but I know they feel like I sold them out since I'm fucking with you."

"Listen, ma, I know you love your job, but you 'on't need that shit. I have more money than you'll be able to spend in a lifetime, even with your lavish spending."

"Boo, I know you got me, but for real, Alijah, I love what I do, and I'm good at it. Even as a little girl, I loved doing hair. Not only that, I'm independent. I love my own money, even though I love spending yours."

"Ms. Independent . . . That's what I love and respect about you, ma. A lot of broads your age wit' your type of body just lined up waiting to hit the jackpot with a dope boy, but not you. Even though I keep you laced, you still like getting your paper."

"Damn, boy, you just gave a whole speech," I said, then started to laugh.

"Wipe those tears, girl. We gon' make it. The only ones that can separate us is us. Don't you forget that."

"I know, I know. I just want to enjoy life without the drama."

"That's what I'm talkin' 'bout," he said, then opened the glove compartment and pulled out some papers. "Yo, look at this." He handed them to me.

I took a look. It was two first-class tickets to Jamaica.

"Oh my God, baby," I screamed. "When we leaving?"

"Two days from now."

The day before Thanksgiving we landed at Norman Manley International Airport in Kingston. It was definitely an experience. I was hot and frustrated, and we had to wait in a long-ass line to claim our luggage. I was happy I was with Alijah who took control of the entire situation.

We finally made it to our hotel. It was beautiful and very clean. They treated us like royalty. Our room was facing the ocean—*that* was a sight to see. I quickly showered, got dressed, and walked out on the patio to get a whiff of fresh island air.

Our first night, we took it easy. We ate dinner and went to the pub where we sat back with drinks and listened to the soft melodies of old-school reggae. I was so at ease, like all my worries were gone. I looked across the table at my boo. I realized at that moment that I loved everything about that man—his walk, his personality, even his arrogance.

"Ma, you good?"

"Yes, I'm just trying to figure out how I got so lucky to have you in my life."

"Nah, you have it backward. I'm the lucky one for real."

"Either way, I don't want it to end."

"Ma, you know I'm not goin' nowhere. You my Bonnie to my Clyde."

"Only you keep forgetting something . . ."

"What?" he asked with a dumb look on his face.

"You're still married to Shayna."

"Ma, that's a dead issue. I'm not gonna get into all the info right now, but fuck that bitch."

I wanted to scream. My nosy ass couldn't help but wonder what happened for him to speak about her like that. Maybe he just saw that bitch for the poison she really was. Anyway, I'd be waiting on him, so we could really make it official.

We went for a ride around the city of Kingston and then decided to call it a night. When we got back to the room, I got ready for bed while he talked on the phone.

Twenty minutes later, there was a knock on the door. Alijah answered it. A tall, dark-skinned Rastafarian man walked in. They gave daps and hugged, so I figured they were old buddies. Alijah introduced him as Trevor. We exchanged greetings, and they departed to the patio.

As I lay in bed waiting on my boo to join me, I started to think about Mo'. I wondered what she was doing at that moment. She wasn't thrilled that I was taking the trip. She kept complaining that she couldn't run the shop by herself, but I knew better.

Lately, I felt like she was catching feelings. I checked her about it, especially her new attitude toward my man. Whenever he said hello, she wouldn't answer. Instead, she rolled her eyes and walked off. Alijah really didn't pay her no mind, which was good because I would be fucked up if he found out about her eating me up.

The rest of our stay in Jamaica was the most fun I ever had in my life. We went to beaches, parties, and smoked some good weed. I didn't want to go when it was time to leave. On our plane ride back to the States I got lost in my thoughts. It was crazy how we took certain things for granted; those are the same things they would kill for. I really saw why Alijah pushed the way he did because of where he came from.

He slept the whole plane ride. I felt like something was bugging him. Our last day in Jamaica, he was very withdrawn. I did not ask any questions. Maybe he was just worn out from all the partying we did. I closed my eyes and fell asleep on his shoulder.

Shayna Jackson

Alijah Jackson, the man that I married four years ago, had turned into a selfish bastard. If I had any doubts before about what I was going to do, they were all gone now. He was going to pay for every bit of anguish that he bestowed on me.

I lied to Markus that I was going to divorce Alijah and be with him, so he gave me all of Alijah's financials. I felt sorry for the fool, but I had to include him in my plot.

I got up bright and early; I had a busy day ahead. I got dressed in a Liz Claiborne striped suit with some nice heels and applied minimal makeup. I was going for the corporate look. I parked on Main Street and walked into the building with confidence. After showing them my ID right away, I spotted two officers standing by the metal detector.

"Hello, good morning. My name is Shayna Jackson. I need to speak to the head guy. What's his name . . . Kevin?" I asked, pretending I didn't really remember the man's name. That was just a show. I did my homework before I pranced in there; that way, I knew who I was dealing with.

"Give me your ID and wait here," the white guy said, then disappeared down the hall.

The Latino officer tried to make small talk. "It's a beautiful morning, isn't it? It's not too cold."

"Hmm. It will be even better when I get to speak to your boss."

He gave me a look that said, "Bitch, what's your problem?"

I kept my focus on my situation. I didn't give a damn about the weather, whether it rained, snowed, or sleeted. Then the white guy came back out front.

"Ma'am, come this way with me."

I followed him through double doors that led to an office with a huge mahogany table. I guessed that was the room that they used to discuss criminal activities. Sitting at the head of the table was a huge white guy with a shiny baldhead. When he stood, he had to be about six foot nine. He looked like a giant when standing up beside his colleagues.

"Ms. Jackson, welcome." He shook my hand with a tight grip.

"Thank you, Commissioner Sanders." I sat across from him.

"I see you did your homework."

"Yes, I did. I like to know who I'm dealing with."

"So, what brings you to my neck of the woods?"

"Before I begin, I need some type of confirmation that I will not be implicated in any of this."

"You have to give me more than that to go on. What's the nature of the information?"

"All due respect, Commissioner, you're not dealing with no slouch. I've been an attorney for nine years and have dealt with the law on several occasions. Excuse my French, but you all are a set of crooks. You use people to your advantage, then cast them out for the sharks to get afterward."

"Ms. Jackson, I'm a very busy man, so unless you have some good dirt for me, get the fuck out of my office."

I saw that he wanted to be a hard ass; wait until he saw what I had. "Well, fine. I have drugs and murder happening right here in Richmond."

"May I ask how you know this?"

"I thought you'd never ask. I'm married to the head nigga in charge of the operation."

"Oh, that explains it. Give me a name."

"Nope, you going to do it on my terms, and I will hand him and his crew to you on a silver platter." I saw his eyes light up. "I knew you'd see things my way after all."

"Well, I see that you're a woman that knows what she wants."

"Definitely, but you can take your eyes off my breasts now. I have everything that I need right here in this briefcase, but here is the document that you need to sign first, offering me immunity." I shoved the document to him.

I have seen a lot of wives catch conspiracy cases with their husbands, just from knowing or being around them, so before I started singing like a parrot, I made sure he offered me immunity from any future prosecution by any state or federal government.

He called in two of his colleagues to join him. I told them everything from the first day I had met Alijah and his friends, his operation in New York, all the conversations that I overheard about all the murders that they committed, and that he was the top supplier in Richmond. Last but not least, I told them about the terrible killings over in the East End.

I didn't want to come off as the scorned wife, so I told them about his infidelity and that I wanted to move on, but I was in fear of my life. I even busted out crying. Agent Sanders fell for the bait and handed me some tissue.

"Ms. Jackson, I do sympathize with you. A good woman like yourself shouldn't have to live with a murderer like your husband. You deserve better. I assure you my office is going to investigate all these allegations and gather information to go in front of the grand jury. However, I need you to do me a favor."

"What? Name it . . . anything . . . I can't live like this no more." I wept some more.

"I understand. I'm going to need you to play your position. Don't give him the slightest idea that we're on to him. We wouldn't want him to flee our jurisdiction."

I gave him the tape and all the documents; then we shook hands. I left, feeling satisfied with myself.

***

I was unable to reach Markus for days. I went by his house. His car was parked outside, but his lights in the house were turned off. At first, I thought that he was ducking me, so I pulled to the corner and waited for a few hours and still no action. He just disappeared into thin air. That was kind of weird. He had never missed a meeting with me. I didn't know what to make of it, but if I didn't hear from him, I was going to file a missing person report.

It was strange how Alijah accused me of infidelity; then I told him it was Markus. Then Markus just disappeared. I knew I was wrong for that, but I was scared what he might have done if I had not given him Markus's name.

I called Sanders to see how things were coming along. That prick had the nerve to tell me he needed more. He wanted me to wear a wire. See, that's what I was talking about. Those damn pigs didn't care how they obtained evidence, even if it meant putting my life in danger. I wasn't no fool. If Alijah ever suspected that I was setting him up, I'd be on the next news flash. I flatly turned him down. I did my part and gave him everything that he needed to put Alijah out of business. All he needed was to get off his lazy ass and put the final touches on.

I went to the bank and tried to get two hundred thousand. At first, they gave me a hard time, talking about they needed both signatures. I told them my husband was unavailable, and we had an emergency. I started to bawl and create a scene until they finally gave in. Those people were some damn fools. When they wanted your business, it was easy to put it in, but when you wanted it out, it was a big fucking problem. I decided to get the rest once they picked Alijah up.

I was going to be all right when it was all said and done. I was going to come out on top. I might be divorced, but I'd be rich. The thought of all that money gave me an instant tingling between my legs.

I filled out a missing person report on Markus a week later. I even went as far as calling his mom. She hadn't seen or heard from him either, which was strange because they spoke almost daily. I had a bad feeling in my stomach. I made a call to Sanders and told him about my concern. He promised me he would check into it for me.

I called Alijah's phone and got no answer. I hadn't spoken to him since the incident at the house when he beat my ass. At this point, I didn't care. It was strange that his business phone was turned off; maybe he got a new phone. Hmm. I knew one person that would've known. I dialed his mom's number.

"Hey, sugar," she greeted me.

"Hey, Ma."

"How you doin', chile? Haven't heard a word from you since you left the funeral."

"I know, Ma, but your son been on his rampage again." I rubbed it in.

"Dat bwoy never learn. I keep telling him, but he hardheaded."

"I know, Ma. I tried everything. I really thought it was goin' to be different when we moved." I started boo-hooing.

"Sugar, dry dem darn tears. It's his loss. God knows you're a good woman. You don't deserve this."

"Listen, Ma, he moved out and went to live with the girl you met."

"Really? He never mention anything. He called me last week to tell me he was going home for a week."

"Home?" I asked, confused.

"Yes, chile, home to Jamaica. You know he love to visit every now and then."

By then, I was spitting fire. This motherfucker left the country without me knowing. I bet money he took that bitch with him. I should've known when I hadn't seen him lately. I quickly rushed her off the phone. I promised her I would come visit soon, which was a damn lie. By the time her son got back, he'd be arrested, and I was going to be long gone, far away from him and his stupid-ass mother.

I finished work early; didn't have much to do. I had a big client for next week, so I left the paralegal all the paperwork I gathered before I left. After that, I headed home. I was ready for a drink.

Traffic was heavy leaving the city. I suddenly realized that I had no gas in my car, so I pulled over to the Texaco. I got out and used my card to pay for my gas. The next thing I heard was a loud crash. A car had run into the back of my car. I took my card out and hurried over to inspect the damage. That's when I saw a young, skinny-looking woman emerge from behind an old Toyota Camry. So, you're telling me that sick-ass bitch just ran her hoopty into the back of my brand-new Benz, and more than likely, she had no insurance. Just my fucking lucky day.

She got out of her hoopty. "I'm sorry, miss. I just forgot to put the car in park. I am so sorry."

"That you are. I hope you have some fucking insurance on this piece of shit you driving." I kicked her car with my heels.

Instead of responding, she busted out crying. "Please, miss, don't call the police. I–I 'on't have no license. I was staying with my boyfriend, and he kicked me out."

Something about her story caught my attention. Maybe it was the fact that I was going through the same pain by a no-good nigga.

"Don't cry. It'll be all right; just go on home."

"Home? I don't have no home. I was staying with him, and he put me out."

I wanted to get back in my car and drive off, but something inside of me told me to listen to her sob story. The attendant in the gas station came out and saw what was going on.

"Miss, do you need me to call the authorities?"

"No, I got it under control."

"All right. Could you move your vehicles, so the other customers can get to the pump?" He shot me a strange look, then walked back into the store.

I examined the severity of the damage. It didn't look that bad. I'd have to take it to the dealer; they'd handle it for me.

"You need to get yo'self together. Let's get these cars out of the way. We can pull over there by the phone booth," I said, pointing my finger.

I got in my car and pulled to the side of the building. I sensed there was more to her story than meets the eye. She seemed high off something, and it wasn't life.

"We did all this talking, and I didn't introduce myself. I'm Shayna Jackson."

I would've extended my arm for a handshake, but not with her hands. The whole time she was crying, snot kept running down her nose, and since she didn't have any tissue, she used her hands to substitute.

"Hi, I'm Neisha," she said with a look like she was trying to recap some information in her delirious mind.

"Did you say Shayna Jackson?" she asked.

"Yes, the one and only," I bragged.

"You married to Alijah Jackson, the big man in Richmond?"

I wasn't going to answer her question, but I wondered how the hell she knew him. Hell, no, I hope he wouldn't stoop *that* low as to put his dick into something looking like her ass.

"No, it's not what you're thinking. We're not messing around, but my best friend Sierra is."

The bitch suddenly got my full attention. "Gurl, stop lying. You and Sierra best friends?" I tried to sound all ghetto.

"Well, not no more, but we used to be best friends until she start messing around with his ass."

"How is that? If y'all so tight, you all let a man come between your friendship?"

"Easy. She got all high and mighty when he started to spend all that dough on her and bought her that house."

"Girl, give me some of that good shit you're smoking. He didn't buy her no house. She lives over there by Creighton Projects or something like that." I looked at her for confirmation.

"You mean Creighton? That's old news. She moved outta there a couple of months ago. I'm telling you, he bought her a house over in the West End—furniture and all. I was with her."

"Hmm, gurl, that's a penny compared to what he be spending on me." I tried to downplay the seriousness of this new information she just threw my way.

After that, she wouldn't shut up. Especially after I told her I'd give her $2,000 so she can get an apartment and fix herself up, even though I had little faith that she was going to find a place to live. Most of it—if not all of it—was going to the nearest dope man.

I stayed a little longer, making small talk with her. Sierra must've done her something terrible because she dogged her out without even catching a breath. She went as far as giving me the address to the house. Damn, that was easier than I thought. For two grand, I got all the information that I needed. It was crazy how things turned out. A simple accident turned into two strangers chatting away like lifelong friends.

I had a motive, and she had hers, even though she never disclosed what it was. Although a fool could tell, it was nothing good.

"Hello, Commissioner Sanders, we need to talk ASAP. I'll meet you in the office in about twenty minutes."

Chapter Fifteen

Alijah Jackson

I was in deep sleep when we landed because all I felt was Sierra elbowing me in my side.

"Damn, we're here already?"

"Yea, baby, wipe yo' mouth."

I wiped my mouth just to make sure I wasn't dribbling.

"Gotcha!"

"Yo crazy ass betta stop playin' wit' me."

"Yea, boy, whatever," she said, smiling.

We got off the plane, claimed our luggage, and headed out of the terminal. I felt well rested, but knew as soon as I got back to Richmond, the stress was going to creep right back up on me. I wished that the vacation could've lasted forever, especially with my girl.

My boys were waiting for us by the time we got outside.

"Whaddup, Boss?" they said in unison.

"Shit, taking it easy."

"Yea, yo' ass done got black as coal," Dre joked.

"Yea, that good ole sun."

"Sierra, what's good wit'cha?" Chuck asked.

"Nada; just tired."

"C'mon, let's get you home then."

We all got in Dre's Suburban truck and headed for Richmond.

"Yo, cut the heat on, B."

"I gotcha, partna."

"You better, homie," I said, laughing my ass off. "I missed y'all, though. No joke 'bout that."

"That's what I'm talkin' 'bout," I said after Chuck handed me a blunt.

"Nah, nigga, you should've brought back some a that good ole ganja."

"Yea, right, with all those jakes and sniffing dogs? Shit, I'm good."

"Oh yea, my bad."

Then there was complete silence on the ride home. I kind of felt excited to be back home. I was ready to get back into the flow of things. Time was money, and I was wasting time. When we got to the house, Sierra went to bed, and me and the guys went into my office. I was eager to discuss some B.I. ASAP.

It was still early in the night, so we decided to roll out. I got my burner and placed it in my waist. It was back to the regular; got to stay strapped. I set the alarm, and we headed out the door.

Suddenly, I felt a gun in my back, and I tried to reach for mines.

"Lemme get that from you," a voice said.

Then, out of nowhere, cars came rushing from all angles up the driveway. They were everywhere.

"Get down now," a big burly dude said.

"Get down! Richmond Police, Richmond Police Department."

I obeyed the order even though I wanted to say, "Suck my dick." They had Chuck and Dre in the same position. The same big pig placed handcuffs on me, then helped me up off the ground. I kept my cool even though my heart was racing. This was my first time getting cuffed. I wasn't scared, though; I was mad as hell.

I heard Chuck going off on them. They dragged him down the driveway into the police cruiser. I saw fire in Dre's eyes as he watched what they were doing to his partna. All I heard Chuck keep saying was "Fuck y'all bitch-ass niggas." I felt the same way, but I was not going to make a bad situation worse.

The big pig came back to where I was standing. "Alijah Jackson, you're under arrest for murder."

"Who tha fuck I murder?" I cut him off before he could finish reading me my rights.

They put us all in separate cars. I didn't know what the fuck was going on or what murder he was referring to. I had been merking niggas since I was fifteen. How was I supposed to know which one they're referring to?

On my way to see the magistrate, I was hurting. Not so much for myself, but for Sierra. Don't get me wrong, I knew I was in a fucked-up situation, but I felt more for her. Before we left, I saw her peeping through the blinds. I was happy that she didn't run out there like most chicks would've done, because if she did that, they would have had a reason to go up in there. I definitely didn't want that. I couldn't risk her catching a charge behind me.

The magistrate denied my bond. The bitch said the charge was too serious. I was fuming by then, but I kept my cool. I was fingerprinted, searched, and given a blanket. They placed me in a cage that was cold and smelled like stale piss. I was glad my stomach was empty; if not, I would've hurled.

They gave me a phone call, so I called Shayna, so she could get to the bottom of the shit. The magistrate mentioned that I was charged with murdering Anthony Smith and a couple of other names. I knew then it was Li'l Tony. She needed to get to the bottom of it. I knew damn well ain't no way I could possibly be implicated in that nigga's murder. I knew they didn't have anything on me; they were just fishing. But, I couldn't help but wonder why my name was involved in the first place.

I dialed Shayna's number but got no answer from the house or her cell phone. I knew we weren't fucking with each other, but fuck it. I was locked up for murder.

I called Saleem right away. "Yo, bruh, it's me. Listen, I'm in the belly a' the beast. Don't know what's going on . . . don't know what's going on . . . but I need you to find out. Call wifey; get her down here by nine-thirty tomorrow morning."

"Gotcha. Keep yo' head up, brotha. I'm on it. I'll see you soon."

"Jackson, your time is up," the guard yelled.

"Man, I got to go."

"Peace, my brotha."

I walked back into my cell, trying to rack my brain for information on what they had on me and what they were charging Chuck and Dre with. No one saw us that day. Something wasn't adding up. And how did they know Sierra's address? Those were all questions that I needed to know the answers to. I tried my hardest to doze off, but with the clicking of the cells and the stench coming from the cell, I just ended up with a migraine.

I jumped up when the sheriff deputy called my name.

"Mr. Jackson, you have court this morning."

"Did my lawyer show up yet?" I asked.

"Not yet, but I'll let you know as soon as he gets here."

"It's a she. Shayna Jackson, pussy hole."

He didn't answer. He turned around and walked away.

It was my time to see the judge. The courtroom was crowded, but I spotted my baby girl sitting in the front row. I read her lips as she whispered that she loved me. I felt a little better seeing her face. It was strange that I didn't see Shayna. Instead, I saw a young, black dude in an expensive suit approach the desk.

"Your Honor, I'm Keith Johnson, Mr. Jackson's attorney."

Who the fuck was that dude, and where was Shayna's bitch ass at? Well, fuck it. He was there, so let's see if he could work magic and get me the fuck out of there.

I should've known better. It wasn't going to work in my favor. Word in the street was that Judge Shakes was the most racist pig in the court system, and here my black ass was standing up there with another black nigga in a nice suit trying to ask to set me free, when in reality, most niggas bond out and never showed back up. Why was I any different? Can't kill a man for trying.

I returned to my cell with a few other cats that were in the same boat as myself—denied bond. I couldn't believe that clown-ass judge denied me bond, claiming I was a flight risk. I wasn't going to trip, though. Instead, I took it like a trooper.

It was evening time before I got processed. Immediately after that, I was given an orange jumpsuit, washcloth, towel, a roll of toilet paper, and a mat to sleep on. I was on the second tier G2. When I walked in my cell, my bunky wasn't there, so that gave me time to get my shit situated and get my thoughts together.

I jumped straight on the phone. I saw niggas gritting on me, and I gritted right back at them to let them know I was in no mood to be fucked with, especially with all the frustration that I had built up in me. I could really punish a nigga. I was known for gunplay, but I was also a beast with them hands.

I dialed Shayna's number. Still no answer. Both her phones were going straight to voice mail. I hung up and dialed Sierra's number. She picked up.

"Whaddup, ma?"

"You a'ight, baby?"

"Yea, ma, I'm a'ight. You know a nigga got to maintain."

"Listen, boo, I'll be down there this evening. I miss you so much."

"I miss you too, ma, but listen, I need you to get on top of shit for me. A'ight?"

"Yea, what's up?"

I had her call Shayna's number on three-way. She still wasn't picking up. It was like she just dropped off the face of the earth. I wondered what the fuck she was doing. I almost regretted killing Markus because he would be on top of shit for real.

I also called Saleem. He was handling everything. Everything was under control out there. My fifteen minutes ended fast, but I called back three other times. I was really missing her, and her crying didn't help any. I wished I could've held her and told her it was going to be all right, but the truth was, I didn't know what those fools really had on me and wouldn't know until the fake Johnnie Cochran came to see me.

On my way back to my cell, a couple of niggas approached me, basically riding my dick. I didn't recognize not one of them. They were just going by word of mouth. Which was cool, so they should know I wasn't nothing nice. I kicked it with them for about five minutes; then I jetted off.

It had been a long day. Plus, my wifey was on her way. I walked back to my cell, where a stout dude was sitting on the top bunk.

"What's up, my man?" I tried to be polite. If we were going to be sharing the cell, the least I could do was be polite.

"Whaddup, youngin'?"

I recognized right away he was from D.C. They the only cats that refer to niggas as youngin'. I used to go out to Southeast D.C. to handle business with some Jamaican cats out there. I never really got personal with them because they came off as a bunch of confused niggas. They were right in the middle, so they didn't know if they wanted to ride with New York or Virginia cats.

"This your first time in, youngin'?"

"Son, no disrespect, but my name is Alijah. I prefer you address me that way."

"Word. Well, mine is J-Rock. I would like for you to use it," he said with a grin on his face.

I wasn't stuttin' him. I had just met him, and I already liked him. It was already chow time. I wasn't hungry, so I stayed in the cell. I took a shower, got dressed, and waited to hear my name called for visitation.

I heard someone holler, "Dude, you on TV."

I paid it no mind.

A little, yellow-skinned dude with missing teeth peeped in my cell. "Yo, bro, I was talkin' to you."

I had no idea what that fool was talking about, but I was curious to see. I walked over to where everyone was crowded around the television that was on full blast. Sure enough, there I was on TV, along with Chuck and Dre. This was outside of the crib. Damn, the whole time we were on TV, and we didn't even know.

I tried to listen to what the DA was saying, but it was too late. Whatever he said had the crowd hollering at me and looking at me crazy. I knew those niggas were from Richmond and probably from Creighton. I knew I was outnumbered, but I didn't give a fuck. I was going to defend mines. Luckily, for them, no one jumped out there, which was good because only God knew how it was going to end up.

"Alijah Jackson, you have a visit. Please have your armband on," the deputy announced.

I was on point. I was hyped up to see my baby girl. I watched as she walked toward my window. I knew I had to be strong for her. I picked the phone up.

"What's good, ma?"

"Boy, you. I couldn't wait to get up here."

"Yea, you still beautiful."

"Boy, you a trip. You acting like you been gone for a while."

"I haven't? It sure feels like it," I said sarcastically. "Nah, ma, I'm just missing you."

"Me too, baby. I couldn't sleep last night. Mo' came over for a while, and we kicked it until she went home."

"Ma, you and Mo' is gettin' a little bit too tight. Let me find out she like you."

"Boy, please, you play too much," she said with an attitude.

We ended up talking about other things. There wasn't too much we could talk about on the phone because we already knew all our conversation was been recorded. In the end, our thirty minutes was up. I saw the pain in her eyes that I caused her. I wish I could've erased all her pain that I brought upon her, but it was too late for that. I just had to keep the faith and hope for the best.

Sierra Rogers

I thought I was dreaming when I heard all the commotion outside. My first instinct was to be nosy, so I rushed over to my bedroom window to see what all that chaos was that was taking place outside. What I saw was straight out of the show *The Wire*. Richmond PD had their guns drawn while Alijah and his boys lay flat on their stomach.

I wanted to rush out there and get my baby, but you know I wasn't no stranger to that type of police brutality, so I kept my calm. The last thing I needed was for them to come up in the house. Alijah had about four burners up in here, so I sat back and watched it play out.

The next few minutes were the worst fear of every hustler's wife who had ever witnessed her man hauled off to jail. "Noooo!" I yelled as they drove off into the dark streets. I didn't know what to do. I ran in the closet, took out the burners, and ran down to the basement. I hid them behind the hot water boiler. It wasn't a good hiding place, but for the time, it would do.

By the time I went back upstairs, all the police cars were gone. I was still uneasy. I didn't know what was going on and if they were going to come back with a search warrant. I sat on the couch with my head on my lap and busted out crying. Damn it! We just came back from our vacation, and now that shit happened.

I looked at the clock. It read 9:45 p.m. It was still early. I had to find out where they took him to and on what charges. I called 411 so I could get the number for the Richmond City Jail. I was going to get my baby out ASAP.

"Hello, Richmond City Jail. May I help you?" an older woman answered the phone.

"Yes, I'm calling to see about Alijah Jackson. What are his charges, and how much is his bond?"

"Hold on a second, ma'am, so I can check . . . Yes, he's here, and he's charged with first-degree murder and conspiracy to commit murder. He has no bond."

I didn't bother to thank her; I just hung up the phone.

"Murder," I just kept repeating to myself.

I felt bad that I didn't check on his boys, but their bitches needed to be checking like I was. I kept pacing back and forth, trying to contemplate my next move.

I decided to call Li'l Mo'. Maybe she could give me some advice.

"Bitch, when did you get back?"

"A few hours ago, and shit hit the fan."

"What you mean?"

"They locked Alijah and his boys up outside of the house."

"For what?"

"They said murder. I 'on't kno' what the fuck going on, but I need you to come over here ASAP. Help me figure this shit out."

"I'm on the way."

"Sorry I took so long. I was all the way out West Broad wit' Jonte's fine ass. Bitch, you owe me 'cause I had to take a rain check, and he was mad as hell that I left before he got some pussy."

"I'll make it up to you, but I couldn't deal with this by myself. I know you been in this type of situation before when Troy caught his case."

See, Troy was Mo's boyfriend before he caught a federal case, and they sent him away for twenty-five years for twenty kilos of cocaine. She still sends him money and goes to see him on the regular, but other than that, she been moved on to the next dope boy.

"Well, you need to go see him in the morning. Do you know if he has a lawyer?"

"I don't know nothing, but the lady did say he has court in the morning."

We sat down and tried to figure out who it was he was supposed to have killed, but it was useless, for real. I didn't know much about Alijah; only what he wanted me to know. I prayed to God he wasn't that careless to get caught up in that mess. I knew being in love with a nigga in the game, there were only two outcomes: him doing a bid or cooling six feet under. I hoped neither one was Alijah's fate.

That night I was glad Mo' came over, because without her company, I'd have lost my mind. Any other time if we're alone, we'd be going at it, but we didn't this time. We just lay there, smoked a blunt, and drank a glass of Alizé. I lay in her lap as she rubbed my back while I vented about Alijah.

I wanted her by my side, but she had to go open up the shop. We still had clients' hair to do, and I did feel bad that I wasn't there to handle my share of the responsibilities. Before she left, I placed all the burners in her trunk. She was going to be watching them until I was sure what was going on. My gun was registered, so that wasn't a problem.

By 8:30 a.m., I was dressed and on my way out the door. I was the first person up in Courtroom A, where Alijah's case was on the docket. It seemed like forever for his name to be called. Even though he had on a bright-ass orange jumpsuit, baby boy still looked sexy. I gave him a big smile, even though I was hurting to see him like that. They had my baby shackled like he was an animal.

A young black brother stood up when Alijah walked in. I knew right then that he wasn't no court-appointed lawyer by the way he walked with arrogance, and he spelled money from head to toe with his expensive suit and gator shoes. He resembled a young Johnnie Cochran. I scooted up closer on the bench. I was trying to catch every piece of info that Judge Shakes was spitting out. His lawyer was also thorough with his words, but the prosecutor wouldn't let up. They went blow-for-blow. In the end, his bail was denied.

I saw the disappointment on Alijah's face. I got really heated when I saw the faggot-ass DA smiling with his partner. I wanted to cuss him and the judge out. My man was innocent. How could they do this to him? Luckily, I caught myself. I had to keep a straight head. I couldn't get in trouble too. I had to stay focused. I had to be strong. That's what a bad bitch did for her man.

I stayed back and had a talk with his lawyer.

"Hello, I'm Sierra, Alijah's girlfriend." I stretched my arm out and shook his hand.

"Hello, I'm Keith Johnson."

"Let's get to the point. What they have on him?"

"Well, I just got a call by Brother Saleem this morning, so I really didn't get to talk to Alijah or the DA as yet. All I know right now is that he's been charged with multiple counts of murder."

"So, by when will you know something?" I asked. I hated that I was coming off as arrogant, but this wasn't the time to get all cordial. I just needed to know what was really good.

"Well, it's still early. I'll be staying behind so I can meet the DA and get all the details and get a copy of the charges. Give me your number. I'll give you a call as soon as I learn something."

"I need to get your number also," I demanded.

In my mind, all lawyers were crooks who got overpaid to use their mouthpiece. The way I was good with mine, I should've went to law school.

I left the courtroom feeling broken. Every hope that I had that morning when I left the house had vanished. I felt like crying. I really thought the judge would've given him a bond. I totally forgot that it was the commonwealth state. They made up their own damn rules.

I stood by the elevator waiting to go to the parking garage. People were standing around me talking. I felt out of it until I heard two voices behind me. When I looked back—I be damned—it was the little homo DA who stopped my man's chance of walking out today.

I wasn't just saying he was a faggot to be funny, but I been around Charley long enough to recognize one of his homies. He had on a tight burgundy suit with what seemed like a pair of Payless loafers, and his hair on his head was slicked down going to the back.

The little faggot had the nerve to smile at me when we got on the elevator. Sure, I smiled back, because without him knowing, he just gave me the perfect idea to help my man. I walked off the elevator feeling rejuvenated. I had to hurry home so I wouldn't miss Alijah's phone call.

I sat by the phone waiting on him to call. See, a bitch like myself should've been out shopping or getting my nails done, but instead, I was sitting in the house feeling sorry for myself.

The phone finally rang. I pressed five and accepted the call. I thought he would've sounded down, but instead, he sounded sexy as usual. I knew him. He was true to the game. I was shocked when he asked me to three-way him to that bitch Shayna, but I didn't trip. I knew the fucked-up situation that he was in. It was not the time to get all jealous.

I swallowed my pride and dialed her number. There was no answer. I wondered what was going through his mind, because in my mind, I wondered where the fuck that bitch was at in a time like this, when my man's life was on the line. I knew he was disappointed when she didn't answer, but I wasn't going to speak about it. Plain and simple, it wasn't my business.

We talked for a while, all along being very careful what was said on the phone because we both knew that the folks were listening.

I hung up and went to the shop to check in on Mo'. I gave her what little details I had. She encouraged me to keep the faith. She offered to come over and keep me company, but I turned her down. Not that I didn't want to chill with her, I just needed some "me time" to get my head straight and put all the pieces together.

I was one of the first females lined up to see my man. The room was filled with lonely girlfriends and wives trying to visit their man for half an hour. As I glanced around, I could tell the different lifestyles of the ladies. The hustlers' wives were branded out from head to toe, hair done, nails done, and well iced out, while the other bitches were dressed in clothes from Rainbow or Marshalls. I knew I was crazy for sitting there doing some shit like that, but I was nervous and needed something to occupy my mind. For real, no matter what we had on, we were all in the same boat.

I sat patiently as one by one they got called in. I felt a lump in my stomach. I hoped that Alijah didn't forget to put me on his visiting list. I knew I was tripping, but after seeing a young girl get turned back because her baby daddy forgot to put her on his visiting list, that couldn't be me. I wouldn't have left until they let me see his behind, and then I would let that no-good son of a bitch rot in hell.

I was buried deep in thought when they called visitors for Jackson. I hurried over and handed my driver's license to the guard. I watched as he checked the piece of paper in front of him.

"Clear. Go this way." He pointed to the double door.

I was so happy to see Alijah, even though it was behind glass. He looked tired and worn down, like he was carrying the burden of the whole city on his shoulders. I gave him the information that I found out about his boys. They were all facing the same charges for Li'l Tony and his crew. Saleem got them their own lawyers.

I cried the entire time. When it was time for me to leave, I was devastated. I didn't want to leave him in that hellhole. I walked out of the jail with a broken heart and revenge on my mind.

Shayna Jackson

It was plastered all over the television set. They finally picked up Alijah and his cronies. I almost busted out laughing. The way everything played out, I was a little disappointed. I thought the feds were going to be handling the case, not the city police. Oh well, it was better than nothing.

I breathed a sigh of relief. Finally, a bitch can live again. I cleaned out the account. The houses were in my name. He wasn't aware that I knew about all his other accounts. Well, I willingly passed on the information. He won't have any use for all that money anyway. He would be behind bars for the rest of his natural life.

Sanders believed that I should go into protective custody, but I begged to differ. I knew they all thought that Alijah was all high and mighty, but with all that evidence that I gave them, that should ensure him a permanent change of address.

The police still couldn't come up with a valid reason about why Markus disappeared. I knew Alijah had something to do with it. They searched Markus's house and came up empty. They had no evidence of foul play. I told them Alijah had the means to make people disappear. I wasn't going to give up until I found out something to tie him to Markus's disappearance.

I had to admit it. I had feelings for Markus. He was one of the few people that really accepted me for me. In a crazy way, he was the only man that put up with my bullshit. It didn't matter how badly I treated him, he always came through for me. I felt bad that I had him caught up in my greed, but, oh well, someone had to be the fool.

I got me a condo all the way up in Midlothian. I should've left Richmond, but I was going to see it all the way through. Plus, I had some unfinished business to take care of. The movers came and took everything out of the house we had together. I couldn't risk Alijah finding out that I set him up and send someone after me. I held on to the divorce papers until after he got sentenced.

I got me new cell phones. After all, I was still a lawyer, and I had clients that were depending on me to get them off of their charges. I wondered if my husband could afford my fees. Oh well, I will never know. Let's see who's laughing now. He always wanted to run the show. Well, it seemed like the only show he was running was in his cell. I'd seen the hardest of niggas go to jail and turn into another nigga's bitch. Alijah used to call them batty boys. If I was him, I would be careful not to throw that word around freely because gang rape happened on the regular behind those walls.

Chapter Sixteen

Alijah Jackson

Holmes came and hollered at me. He told me they had an eyewitness. They were really tripping. I wondered what that fool had seen and who he was. I knew they were bluffing because the only niggas present when I merked that fool were either locked up or dead. Saleem was the only cat present who wasn't involved, and I knew where we stood. I had never questioned his loyalty, and Chuck and Dre were thoroughbreds. They not new to the game; they were true to the game.

I wasn't feeling what he was spitting out. That nigga fee was over twenty grand, but yet he was actin' like he was gettin' paid by the government.

"Mr. Jackson, things are not looking too good. The DA is telling me that they have a very reliable witness to the killings. Maybe we need to cooperate and cut a deal early."

"What! You sound more stupid than you look. Yo, you get paid to fight this fuckin' case and not sit on your ass talkin' bullshit. You understand, bruh? I'm not pleading out. You tell dem muthafuckas I said it." I got up and flipped the fucking table over.

"Mr. Jackson, I'm sorry if I said something to offend you."

"Listen, pussy hole, do yo' fuckin' job. As far as I'm concerned, this meeting is over." I got up and signaled for the CO.

I left that fool sitting there picking up his paperwork off the floor. I got back to the pod and jumped right on the phone. When Sierra didn't pick up the phone, I slammed it down in frustration.

"Yo, bro, take your time wit' the phone. We need it," a flunky-ass nigga came out his mouth sideways.

I stormed toward dude but was stopped midway by a bunch of dudes. I was ready to rumble, but obviously, they didn't want none of me. They put their hands up in defeat.

"C'mon, celly, it ain't worth it, bro. They'll put yo' ass in the hole, and trust me, it's nuttin' nice. Believe me, I know," he warned.

"'Bout now, I 'on't give a fuck. It's whateva. Niggas don't know who they fuckin' wit' for real, son. I put this on e'erything; the next nigga that come at me sideways, I'ma make an example of."

"Let's go in the cube. You talkin' recklessly. Niggas already know about you. Earlier in chow, a few Church Hill niggas were talking. I heard yo' name, so I pulled closer so I could listen to them. They know you a ruthless brotha. Trust me, they know."

Sierra Rogers

I felt alone in the house. I didn't know something this beautiful would end up feeling so cold. I sat on the bed looking at a portrait of me and Alijah when we first met. They said a picture tells a thousand words.

Christmas was two weeks away. Every year, Neisha and I usually celebrated together, but not anymore. I guess I would end up spending it by myself unless something miraculously happened to set Alijah free. Life was not fair. This was the happiest that I had ever been in my entire life and that happiness was being threatened.

I called his lawyer every damn day. I wasn't going to ease up on him. Shit, he was getting paid damn good, so I was going to let him work for every penny. He wanted me to convince Alijah to cop a plea. Now what kind of shit was he smoking? There was no way in hell I was going to help my man get life in prison.

I never met my grandma, but I heard a lot of good things about her. I heard she was a beautiful woman. I wished I had the privilege of meeting her. It was strange when I had a dream with her in it. I was at home in my living room sitting on the floor crying, and out of nowhere, this lady appeared and sat beside me. She gave me a warm smile; one that would warm up a cold room. I smiled back at her like we had met before. That's when she put her arms around me and spoke in the most comforting tone I'd ever heard.

"Grandbaby, what's the matter?"

"Nana, I'm scared for my friend." I looked at her with eyes of a seven-year-old innocent child.

"Sugar, I see he's a special friend to you, but you have to be strong for him. All your crocodile tears are not going to help him."

I looked at her, trying to figure out what the hell she knew. This was back in the good old days; this was 2006. I kept my thoughts to myself, though.

"You have to be his backbone; fight for him. Put yo' boxing gloves on. Grandbaby, sometimes you have to fight a little dirty to win the battle."

"What are you saying, Grandmama?"

"Sugar, you are very smart young woman. You'll figure it out."

Before I could respond to her, my dream was interrupted by the telephone. I jumped out of my sleep, and like that, she was gone. That was some crazy shit because I had never met her. She died before I was born, but obviously, she was watching over me.

That was Mo' blowing up my phone, but I wasn't in the mood to talk. Instead, I sat there and pondered on what that dream meant.

I hadn't been back to the International House of Beauty since the day that I left, but when I phoned Charley to ask him for a favor, I didn't want to discuss it on the phone, so we decided to meet up at the shop. I honked the horn so he could come outside. I felt weird going up in there. Not that I had a problem, but Jazmine was still up in there, and it was too damn early to hear her damn mouth. Plus, I didn't feel like answering all their damn questions.

"Hey, gurl, you look good."

"You don't look bad yo' damn self," I said to him.

"So, missy, what was so damn urgent? You know I'm a busy man."

"I know, but if I didn't need you, I wouldn't have called you this early."

"Gurlll, I heard about yo' man. That's some sad shit. You know all the niggas in Creighton was partying after he got locked up."

"That's a'ight. They gon' get theirs."

"Sierra, be careful now. I 'on't want nothing to happen to you. You know I fucks wit' yo' crazy ass."

"I know, boo, I fucks wit' you too."

"Gurl, I seen your friend . . . What's her name . . . Neisha. Yea, she fuckin' wit' Jon Jon, and he got her all strung out on that crack."

"What?" I asked, shocked as hell. "Stop lying. She's not getting high. You trippin'."

"Bitch, if I'm lying, I'm flying. You know I got it straight from the nigga's mouth."

I knew he wasn't lying. Now I knew why she was acting so strangely. I didn't tell him that I whupped her ass, so I pretended like I hadn't seen her in a while.

I took him for a drive. I didn't want anyone to overhear our conversation.

"Listen, Charley, I need a big favor from you."

"What, gurl, you need to borrow some money?" He gave me a fucked-up look.

"Nah, I'm good on that end, but seriously, I know you like guys, right?"

"Yea, no disrespect to y'all females, but y'all just not my cup of tea."

"That's cool, but I want you to fuck somebody for me for fifty grand."

"Bitch, what you trying to do. Set me up?"

"Nah, but I wish you'd just shut up and listen." I rolled my eyes. If I really didn't need him, I would say fuck him and put him the fuck out of my car.

"All right, gurl, I'm all ears."

"Listen, I know this dude I want you to put that dick on, but I need you to have it taped."

"Bitch, what? You on some real freaky shit. I didn't know you get down like that."

"Not really, it's strictly business. So, I'll give you twenty-five grand up front and the rest when you give me the tape."

"So, you are telling me that you will give me fifty grand to do what I love to do?"

"Exactly, but you got to be careful because he's the fucking law. If he found out we're setting him up, we're going down for sure," I warned.

"How do you know he's gay, 'cause I don't mess around wit' no straight dude. I'm not ready to die yet."

"No, I'm pretty sure he's a faggot. Trust me, ain't nothing straight about him."

"So, now you going to tell me why you're doing this. Don't you think I have a right to know what's going on?"

"All right, it's the lame-ass prosecutor on Alijah's case. He's trying to give my man life, but I can't just sit back and watch him go out like that. I just need evidence to get leverage over ole boy. I know he's married with three kids, one of whom is playing ball for Virginia Tech. I been following him for days, and he frequents the gay club on Chamberlain Avenue. One night he left with a younger dude, and they went to the motel down the street. Two hours later, they reappeared. He wasn't too cautious. I watched his every move, and I even followed him home."

"I see you have it all figured out. Sierra, I knew you since you was a baby. The whole time you been talking, I was trying to figure out why I would put myself in this predicament, but I know you would ride for me. So, it's not all about the money; it's about me helping a friend out. Plus, I might really enjoy it," he said while laughing his ass off. "Sierra, one more thing . . ."

"What?"

"You can't utter a word about this to anyone. I mean *no one,* 'cause, for real, I fucks wit' them niggas. They my little homies. I wouldn't want word to get out there that I helped an outside nigga, especially a nigga that they beefing with. You know I'm a lover, not a fighter."

"I swear on everything that I love—which isn't a lot—this is between me and you, and my man's life depends on this. My intention is to get him out of jail. I'm going to put the pressure on dude, and I'm pretty sure he'll give in to my demand when he sees how serious I am. If he doesn't, my man won't be the only one without a life. Trust me!"

I dropped Charley off at the shop so he could handle some business because at 8:00 p.m., shit was going to be in motion. I stopped by the bank to get the money. It was most of the little money that I had been saving for a rainy day, but in my book, the storm clouds had burst, and Alijah was worth every penny of it.

I held on to my Coach pocketbook for dear life when I walked out of SunTrust Bank. A nigga would have to kill me before I would give them my money, especially when my man's life depended on it.

I stopped by the shop to see Mo' and see how things were going. I knew my clients were upset with me, but their fucking feelings was not that serious right now. I walked in the shop, and it was empty as hell.

"Girl, what's up?"

"Tired as shit. Where you coming from this early?"

"Had to handle some business for Alijah. You know I'm his errand girl," I joked.

"Anything good yet?"

"Nope."

"Don't give up; something have to happen."

"Thanks, girl. What would I do without you? You been a good friend. I appreciate how you holding this place down while I run around tryin'a handle this shit."

"Don't sweat it. That's what friends are for, and you'd do the same thing for me."

"You got that right, especially these days when bitches don't know the true meaning of friendship. Girl, I forgot to tell you that I think the bitch Neisha had something to do wit' all that shit, because all that shit happened after I gave that bitch my address, *and* I found out that bitch is a crackhead."

"Bitch, now you making up shit."

"I'm dead serious. This bitch is a straight fiend."

"You tellin' me that pretty bitch is sucking on a glass dick?"

"Yes, I got it straight from the Nigga News." That's the name we gave Charley.

"Well, friend, better her than us," she said.

We busted out laughing. It felt really good. It had been days since we sat back and kicked it.

After I left the shop, I went home, showered, and lay down for a while. I really needed that rest. I woke up, got dressed, and headed out the door. I had to stop by the mini mall and buy myself a mini camcorder.

Chapter Seventeen

Alijah Jackson

The days were moving in slow motion, so I stayed up at night and slept most of the day. Sometimes, I would kick it with a few of the older heads or play dominoes and card games just to pass the time.

I still claimed my innocence because they'd never caught a nigga slipping. A lot of cats caught a life sentence because they had diarrhea of the mouth. Shit, I was taking mines to the grave.

Saleem came by to visit. I felt good seeing one of my true homies. He only had words of encouragement for me, and it was all love. He told me that Dre sent word not to worry about nothing; he got it. I knew exactly what he meant by that, but I didn't want my nigga to go out like that. On some real talk, I wouldn't let my man do no shit like that, especially when

I was the one that got them in the situation in the first place. I knew he meant well, but I just wouldn't.

Saleem didn't know what was going with Shayna. Ain't nobody seen or heard from her since the arrest, and I wondered if the niggas did something to her on the strength that they couldn't get to me. It was either that or the bitch skipped town with my money. I wasn't tripping on that little chump change that was in our joint account. My intention was let her keep that anyway.

I was thinking hard lately. If I ended up beating the charges, I was going to move to another state, start over fresh—my wifey and me. I was gon' get my divorce from Shayna and make Sierra the next Mrs. Jackson. I wasn't getting any younger. It was time to make some babies and sit back with the wife and live life a little. Every nigga in the game knew you get in, get it, and get out. If you made the mistake of making a career out of it, you'd end up in prison or six feet under.

Sierra Rogers

I got dressed and headed out the door. I had just gotten a call from Charley; he was chilling with dude. He didn't have any trouble hooking up after all. I paid cash for a room at the Red Roof Inn on Laburnum Avenue. I had no idea how long it was going to take before Charley scored. It might not even happen on the first night, but I was prepared.

I paid a good amount of change for the piece of equipment. I wanted the smallest camcorder that was on the market. Something small enough to be discreet. I read the directions and set it up right above the mirror in the room. I wanted to capture every bit of action that took place in the room. I wiped my prints off everything that I touched in there; then I exited the room through the back exit where I was parked. I got in my car, turned on my music, and prepared for a long night.

My phone rang around 11:30 p.m. I knew it was Charley. He gave me the heads-up that they were approaching the motel. Five minutes later, they pulled up toward the entrance of the motel. I left word at the front desk that my husband was going to be showing up, and I had them give him the keys to the room. Everything went as planned.

I watched as Charley entered the room, and exactly three minutes later, ole boy entered.

I scooted back in my seat. Only God knew how long of a wait it was going to be. I lit up a blunt, but it was some straight garbage that tasted like green bush, so I put it out. I was used to smoking the good weed.

Around two in the morning, my phone rang.

"Yo, I'm on my way home," Charley said.

"All right, I'll see you in a few."

That was my cue to follow him. Dude pulled out, then Charley. Then I followed in pursuit. Dude split onto Broad Street, and we continued on. We had to be careful, so I followed when Charley headed to the south, then pulled into the McDonald's on Hull Street. I pulled by him. I got out of my car and got into the car with him.

"So, how you did?" I asked, even though I was afraid to hear the answer.

"Good. You can't tell by my face expression? Baby boy knows how to get down; got a lot of freak in him."

"Yuck, I didn't wanna know all that."

"My bad, you asked. Here you go."

"Thank you, boo, this mean a lot to me. I am so grateful to you." I hugged him.

"Ahh, ahh, don't get all mushy. Just hand me my cheese, and let me get on my way 'cause ole boy wore me out."

I opened my Coach bag and handed him the money.

"Thank you, boo. Sierra, you already know I'm going to give you the speech to be careful. I'm not getting in your business, but you playing a dangerous game."

"I hear you, boo, but I'm a big girl. I can handle it."

We then went our separate ways.

I waited until the morning to view the video. I felt very optimistic about my man's case because Mr. DA was caught with his pants down, fucking and sucking another man. I almost threw up all over my covers. That nigga was a straight faggot. I shook my head. It was crazy how you could be married to a man, and he was living a double life with other men. He wasn't only cheating. He was living recklessly, picking up younger men in bars, and taking them to cheap motels for sex.

Undercover men were one of the major causes of spreading HIV and herpes in heterosexual relationships. Some sick thoughts ran through my head. I would torture a nigga if I ever found out he was living that foul.

I spoke on the phone with Alijah. He sounded a little down. Jail walls could break the hardest of niggas. I tried to comfort him, but I knew it was useless. I tried to be strong for him, but inside, I was hurting my damn self.

I was famished. I hadn't really been eating since all the chaos. Mo' came over for dinner, so I baked some chicken and cooked macaroni and cheese. We ate and drank some Alizé, smoked about three blunts of some Haze, then had sex. I needed to relieve some stress. I even ate her pussy too. I had to pinch myself to make sure it was me. I never imagined in a million years that I would be eating on another chick's pussy, but it was irresistible after finger fucking her on numerous occasions. I had to give it to her; she had some wet, tight pussy. I was happy that I didn't have close neighbors because we went at it like some wild animals in the wilderness.

I called Alijah's lawyer to see if anything changed and to see when his next court date was. I asked if he needed more money, because even though I was down to my last dime, a bitch didn't care if I had to sell pussy to help my nigga out. That's when he told me that

Dre was copping to the charges. I wasn't a bit surprised; they seemed loyal to Alijah. I had a feeling Alijah wasn't going to let it go down like that. Before I hung up, I asked him for the DA's number.

I called and made an appointment. I also lied saying that I was an attorney.

I chose to wear a dark-colored suit by Liz Claiborne. I put on a push-up bra to reveal my cleavage. I was ready to get things accomplished. Then I called a taxi. I didn't want to use my car in case things didn't turn out too well.

I sashayed into the DA's office at 610 Main Street, Suite 604.

"Good morning, ma'am, I'm here to see Mr. Donald Kazowaski."

"Do you have an appointment?" the receptionist asked.

"Yes, I called yesterday to set it up." I was getting nervous by now and thought about leaving, but it was too late to get all scared. I had to get it done.

"Let's see. What's your name again?"

"Kimani Williams," I lied.

She looked through the appointment book. "Yes, here you are, Attorney Williams. Hold on a second." I watched as she buzzed to let him know I was there. "Have a seat. Mr. Kazowaski will be right with you."

"Thank you." I sat on the plush sofa and picked up a magazine to pass the time, but nothing was registering in my mind.

"What law firm did you say you were from?" this nosy bitch asked.

She knew damn well that I never mentioned a law firm; I only said I was a lawyer. I wondered if she was on to me, but I had something for her. Don't try to outsmart me, bitch. Before I could respond, the faggot walked in.

"Ms. Williams, I'm sorry for the wait."

"It's understandable. I have time." I shot him a fake-ass smile.

"Good, follow me to my domain." He pointed to the door.

I had the wrong perception of what the district attorney's office should be like because his office was the size of a closet. They must not make a lot for fucking up people's lives.

I stood up while he sat in his chair.

"Where do I know you from? You look familiar," he said while searching his mind.

"Let me freshen your memory. A week ago, at the courthouse, waiting on the elevator."

"No, I saw you before."

"Oh yes, in the courtroom when you tried to chew my man up. Alijah Jackson . . . You remember now?"

"What are you doing here? You said you're an attorney."

"Yea, forgive me, I did lie," I said with a straight face.

He put his hand to buzz his secretary, I guess to get me thrown out. I had to act fast.

"Listen, Donald, I believe you need to hear me out before you go any further and embarrass yourself. Do you remember where you were last night between the hours of 9:00 p.m. and 2:00 a.m.?" I said, trying to grab his attention.

It worked because he took his hand off the buzzer. Then he took his glasses off and displayed signs of nervousness. I sat down and told him everything that I knew about him, and most importantly, that I had him on tape.

"So, what do you want from me?"

"I thought you'd never ask. I want all charges dismissed against my man and his friends."

"Are you fucking crazy? I can't do that. I don't have the authority to do that. Plus, we have a solid case against those thugs."

"Probably so, but I need him home. Just like you want to be home with that pretty little wife of yours and those kids that look up to daddy—the man—not the faggot you are."

"You little bitch! I could have you arrested right this minute," he spat.

I got up and walked around to where he was sitting. I leaned over with my breasts in his face, then I gave it to him raw. "Listen to me, you little faggot-ass nigga. You don't want to fuck wit' me. Even if you get me arrested right now, yo' dirty little secret will still be plastered across prime time television by 6:00 p.m. when your pretty little family will be seated at the dinner table."

I dug into my pocketbook, took out the camcorder, and pressed Play. I wanted to fall out laughing when I saw how his facial expression changed from calm and collected to anger and embarrassed. After I thought he'd seen enough, I turned it off and placed it back in my bag.

"No need to be embarrassed. We all have our dirty little secrets that we don't want other people to know about. I'm sorry if I come off as a bitch, but honestly, my back is against the wall, just like yours is."

I didn't think he heard a word that I said. Instead, he buried his face into his hands. I knew he was thinking. He needed to hurry up, because if I ever got caught blackmailing the DA, I would definitely be next door to Alijah.

"So, Mr. DA, what's really good? I don't have a lot of time. While you're sitting there chilling, my man is up in a cold-ass cell."

He put his glasses back on his face. "I'm going to see what I can do about letting the evidence 'disappear.' I can't promise you anything. I have people that I have to answer to, but give me a few hours to get back to you. Can I get your phone number, so that I can reach you?"

"Don't play wit' me. You have until 4:00 p.m. to get your shit in order. I'll call you at exactly 3:59. If you don't answer, our deal is off, and your wife will getting a copy delivered to her residence; then the news station will receive their copy. Do you understand me?"

I knew I was pushing it to go as far as threatening him like that, but I had to emphasize the seriousness of the situation. As I turned to leave, he spoke.

"Ms. Williams, you're playing a dangerous game. I'm well affiliated in this town. Next time, you think about *that* before you prance up in here threatening me this way."

"Donald, you're playing a sick game fucking your wife, and then turning around fucking dudes without a condom. Next time, you consider yourself a nasty, no-life nigga that don't deserve to live."

I walked out without speaking to the bitch at the desk. Fuck her too.

I headed home and lay in my bed. I felt nervous about the move I made today. I knew that was some crazy shit, but I was not thinking rational.

I received mail from Alijah. That nigga was a beast with his words, because by the time I was finished reading, I was crying a river like Justin Timberlake did in that song. At three o'clock, I was hyperventilating, so I drank a glass of Hpnotiq to help calm my nerves. At 3:58 p.m. I had to pee. I went to the bathroom, but nothing came down. I washed my hands and grabbed the prepaid phone that I bought earlier just to make the call.

Nervous, I dialed his office.

"Hello, this is Ms. Williams. So, what's up?"

"Could we meet? The phones are not too safe."

"I agree. Where you want to meet at?"

"How about the library by city hall. We could pretend like we're discussing a case since you're already impersonating a lawyer."

I let his smart-ass comment fly. "All right, see you in a few."

I left the house not knowing what was really going to happen. Dude could've been waiting with the police. I took a deep breath. It was a chance that I had to take.

This time I drove my car. I just wanted to get in and got out. I prayed he had some good news. As soon as I walked in the library, I spotted him. I went over and sat beside him.

"Nice to see you again, Donald," I said like we were old buddies.

"Ms. Williams, you put me in a very tight spot. I'd rather turn you over to the authorities, but I can't put my family or the people that I work with through that type of embarrassment you've threatened."

"Okay, can you please get to the point? I'm not trying to hear this entire sentimental crap." I was getting irritated real fast.

"Bottom line is I took all the evidence from the evidence room. Without it, I have no choice but to drop the case."

I was happy inside, but I held my composure. "When can I expect to have my man home?"

"Not so fast. Could I get the recording, and how can I be sure that you have not already made copies?"

"I'm a woman of my word. You give me what I want, and I'll delete everything I have on you, and we will never cross paths again."

He stood there shaking his head like he wasn't buying my story. Eventually, we exchanged gifts, and I walked out first. I held the package he gave me closest to my heart. I hoped that fool didn't think that I gave him the *only* copy of my security. I had the original just in case he didn't keep up his end of the deal.

I rushed into my house and kicked my shoes off. Then I took my clothes off, got comfortable in the bed, and cut my nightlight on. I took everything out of the envelope. It was a stack of papers and a mini tape recorder. I decided to read the papers first. Page by page, I read all the evidence that the State had on my man and his crew. I was kind of thrown off because the feds did the investigation, so why did the State charge him?

I was halfway through the evidence when it hit me that it was an inside job. They had dates of when he took his trips, the date of Li'l Tony and his crew's murders, even murders that happened in New York.

I almost choked when I saw in bold letters "SHAYNA JACKSON, KEY PROSECUTOR WITNESS." That bitch set Alijah up. I had to read it over and over. I couldn't go no further; I was hurting for Alijah.

I put the paperwork down and turned on the tape recorder, scared for whatever I was about to hear. It *was* Alijah's voice on tape crying, talking about Darryl's death, their childhood, their first drug transaction, and all the niggas that they killed together. I was confused at how the bitch managed to get Alijah slipping like that, without him knowing.

I felt hatred for that bitch. No wonder she went MIA after he got picked up. How was I going to tell him it was his precious wife that was snitching?

My eyes were burning. I was beat—more like shocked and worn out, both mentally and physically.

Alijah's court day was scheduled for December 23rd. I still had my fingers crossed. I wouldn't be partying until Judge Shakes brought his gavel down and dismissed the case. I went to visit Alijah, but I kept quiet about everything, which was hard, but I had to play it safe. I would wait until he came home to tell him the news. I let Saleem in on everything. He was like a father figure to my man, so to me, he was good people.

Alijah Jackson

Every day was the same routine. My lawyer came to visit. He didn't come at me like he did last time. He told me that Dre was claiming everything. I wished I could get word to my nigga not to do that. I already made up my mind to handle it like a soldier. I knew it was probably over for me. I wasn't the type to give up, but what the fuck could I do but try my hardest to fight the charges. I was waiting for the motion of discovery so I could see what they had on me.

I also thought about letting Sierra loose for real. I felt like a burden to her. The last time I saw her, she didn't look like her usual cheery self. She looked like she'd lost weight, and her eyes had bags under them like she had been on the block pulling all-nighters. It was going to be the hardest thing for me to do, but it would be best for her.

I didn't call my mom because I definitely didn't want her to see me like that. It would've broken her heart. I was going to seclude myself from everyone. I just didn't want to hurt them no more.

***

"Jackson, attorney visit," the CO yelled over the intercom.

See, in jail when a nigga hear "attorney visit," it's like a kid getting ready to see Santa Claus. I brushed my grill real fast. I had my hair in a ponytail, and I was ready to go. I pressed the intercom button.

"Yo, I'm ready. Bring yo' ass."

"You really need to watch yo' mouth," he said.

"You need to stop acting like a faggot."

The whole pod burst out in laughter.

"You won't be watching anything when I put your ass in the hole for incident to a staff."

I really didn't want no beef with the COs because I needed the phone, and being on lock-down, you get no privileges.

He placed me in the visitation room, and my lawyer walked in smiling his ass off.

"What's so fucking funny?"

"Damn, bro, give me a break. I believe something good is about to happen. Your court date is moved up to the 23rd at 2:00 p.m. I heard from my source that they're dropping the charges."

"Get the fuck outta here."

"No, I wouldn't make this trip if it wasn't worth it. I called the DA that's handling your case, but he was out for the day. I left a message with his secretary for him to give me a call."

"What 'bout my niggas?"

"Their lawyers were the ones that contacted me and gave me the heads-up."

I sat there shaking my head. It was too good to be true, but seeing was believing.

After he left, I got back to the pod and rushed on the phone. When I told Sierra, she was so excited, even though I told her not to be because it might just be rumors. She kept telling me to claim it, and it would happen.

I totally forgot about me telling her to leave me alone. It felt good to have shorty riding with me. I never experienced true ghetto love until I met her.

I was up bright and early. Even though my court was later on, the COs still be transporting you bright and early. Before I left, I got on my knees and talked to God. I let him know I did some terrible things in my life, but if he watched over me this one time, I would change my ways. I was not sure he heard a word that I said, but that day, I walked into that courtroom with confidence.

When my name was called, I walked into the room. Off top, I peeped Sierra standing beside Saleem. She blew me a kiss, and he nodded at me. I took a quick glance around the room. Still no sign of Shayna. I had no understanding about what the fuck was going on with that bitch. But if everything went as planned, I would be paying her ass a visit.

I stood there with my lawyer, and the same faggot-ass nigga stood up for the State.

"Your Honor, the State moves forward to dismiss the case against the defendant Alijah Jackson due to insufficient evidence."

"Mr. Kazowaski, are you absolutely sure? If you need more time to gather evidence, I will give you an extension, because the truth of the matter is, these are some serious charges," Judge Shakes said in a serious tone.

"The State understands, Your Honor, but it would be unfair to the defendant to prolong this case without sufficient evidence."

"Okay, Mr. Johnson, do you agree with the State?"

"Yes, Your Honor, my client's been through a lot physically and mentally. He's prepared to return to society and his family ASAP."

"Well, Mr. Jackson, it seems to me like you've lucked up, but I have no doubt you're indeed guilty of these charges brought against you. However, in the court of law, my personal opinion doesn't count. You're innocent until proven guilty, and since the State of Virginia fails to prove your guilt, I hereby order all charges against you be dropped. You are free to go."

When that nigga uttered those words "free to go," I just looked at my lawyer and smiled. I felt like Martin Luther King. *Free at last.*

I had to return to jail so I could get processed out. I was ready to go. I was going to drink, smoke, and fuck. I gave my bunky my info so he could holla at me. I was definitely going to look out for him. He was a real cool cat.

It felt good to be back in my own clothes. My baby girl was waiting at the door as soon as I stepped out into the cold December night. She jumped on me so hard I almost lost my balance.

"Ma, take it easy. I'm here," I said, picking her up.

Saleem was waiting in the truck. He gave me a hug when I walked up. "Welcome back, brotha."

"It's good to be back, bruh."

"Let's go home, boo," Sierra said.

Saleem dropped us off at home. I jumped right into the shower. I needed to wash that jail smell off of me. I put on some boxers. I shouldn't have even bothered to put them on because Sierra pulled them right off and gave me some of her bomb-ass head. I missed all that, but I was eager to get up in that wet, tight pussy. I beat that pussy up something terrible, and after I was finished, I held her in my arms. She felt kind of tense; I knew something was up.

"What's up wit' you, yo?"

"Alijah, I got something to tell you, but I don't know how to come out and tell you."

The first thought that ran through my mind was that she fucked another nigga. I wasn't going to front. I would be mad as hell, but I wouldn't leave her. She had proved her loyalty, so I needed her on my team.

"What is it, ma. Spit it out."

Nothing could've prepared me for what came out of her mouth.

Sierra Rogers

I was on time to the courthouse. I was so excited and nervous at the same time. Saleem drove his truck down there. He was a handsome, laid-back Muslim dude, and it was a pleasure to be in his presence. We sat at the back of the courtroom.

I spoke to his lawyer, who gave me the good news. All along I played stupid, like I was unaware of what was about to go down. I listened attentively as the DA asked the judge to drop the charges due to lack of evidence. The judge wasn't too pleased.

Alijah smiled at me as they led him out. He had to go back to jail so he could get processed. I was so happy I hugged Saleem, which took him by surprise because he gave me a confused look.

"My man is lucky to have you in his life."

"Woman, he *owes* you his life."

I didn't respond. I was happy. On some real shit, we owed Charley. Without him, none of it would've been possible.

It would take a few hours before they would let Alijah out, so I headed to the shop to share the good news with my ace. I really kept everything that I did from Mo'. She was my bitch, but this was something that I didn't want too many people to know about. I planned to take it to my grave.

"Hey, chica."

"Hey, boo, how did it go in court?"

"Bitch, they let him go. My man is free at last."

"Stop lying, bitch! What happened? Did they let his boys out too?"

"They'll be out tomorrow. They had different court dates, but they don't have any evidence."

"*That's* what's up. Alijah better appreciate and chill out 'cause them niggas going to be mad as hell."

"I know, girl, I'm just so happy right now. I don't know how to fucking act."

I kicked it for a little while longer until Saleem picked me up and we headed to the Richmond City Jail to pick Alijah up. I saw him as he walked toward the door. I was so excited; I jumped all over him. I was elated to finally have my baby back home with me.

By the time we got home, I was ready to fuck. While he went to the shower, I stripped down to my birthday suit and lay in bed with my legs spread wide open, so he could get a good look at what he had been missing. I didn't waste no time. I got on all fours and straight deep throated every inch of his dick. I guess he was starved for some of my good pussy because he snatched me up and turned me around, so he could fuck me doggie style. He fucked me like he was locked up for a lifetime.

***

I was really happy to have Alijah back home, but I was also nervous about how I was going to approach him with all the evidence that I had. I kept playing different scenarios in my head over and over, and I kept going back to the same conclusion. There was no easy way to say it; the bitch was a snitch, and I'd have to give it to him raw.

I guess that he sensed that something was wrong with me because he started to inquire if I was okay. I knew that it was time to lay it all on the table. No matter how it turned out, he had to know.

"Boo, listen, there's no easy way to say this, but I found out who set you up."

"What you found out? So who tha fuck is it, and why you ain't been said sump'n?"

"Listen, don't fucking get on me. I only found out a few days ago, and I was waiting to tell you when you came home, so don't fucking get no attitude with me," I warned.

"A'ight, yo, spit that shit out now!"

"It's your wife, Shayna. She set you and your boys up."

"Sierra, you trippin', ma. I know you 'on't like her and e'erything, but that's some vicious shit to say 'bout shorty."

I couldn't believe my ears. There I was telling this nigga that his fucking wife set him up, and he was accusing me of not liking the bitch. I felt fucking hurt, but I didn't display no emotion. Instead, I got up and opened my dresser drawer. I pulled out the envelope with all the evidence and handed it to him.

"Before you go off accusing me of being vindictive, here look for yourself. It's all there in black and white."

I got up to walk out of the room so he can have some privacy. No need for me to sit around and watch his feelings get crushed. Then I heard the doorbell ring. I knew I wasn't expecting anyone, but it might be someone Alijah was expecting, so I walked to the door and opened it.

"What the fuck are you doing here, and how the fuck you got my fucking address, bitch?"

"Surprise! I told you we'd meet again."

Pop! Pop! Pop! Pop!

"Alijahhhhhhhhhhhh!" I screamed before everything turned black.

I could hear Alijah yelling, police talking, and me carried off in the ambulance. I tried to talk, touch him, and let him know I loved him, but my words were not coming out. Before I knew it, I was out cold, dreaming of a calm place where there was no pain. I looked around and saw all the familiar faces of my homies that went on to heaven. They were hugging me and welcoming me. I must admit it felt so good, but Alijah was not there, and I needed my man beside me.